'Jamie Guiney's stories feel like classics read by the fireside on dark, winter nights. Tales of ordinary people and their everyday lives are illuminated and elevated by Guiney's keen eye and gentle empathy.'

Paul McVeigh − Author of The Good Son. Winner of The Polari Prize and the McCrea Literary Award. Brighton's City Reads 2016 and World Book Night 2017.

'Evocative, lyrical and touching, The Wooden Hill is a stunning collection. Under Jamie Guiney's pen the smallest detail becomes cinematic; characters breathe; landscapes live. Intensely personal, unflinchingly human, these are stories to savour, lingering long after the end. I adored this compilation.'

Miranda Dickinson − Bestselling author of Fairytale of New York, Welcome to My World and A Parcel for Anna Browne.

Jamie Guiney is a writer from County Armagh, Northern Ireland. His short stories have been published internationally and he has been nominated twice for the 'The Pushcart Prize'.

Jamie is a graduate of the Faber & Faber Writing Academy and has twice been a judge for short story competition 'The New Rose Prize.' His work has been backed by the Northern Ireland Arts Council through several Individual Artist Awards and he has also been chosen by Lagan Online as one of their New Original Writers.

Jamie Guiney

The Wooden Hill

époque press

Published by époque press in 2018
époquepress.com

The right of Jamie Guiney to be identified as the author
of this work has been asserted in accordance with section
77 of the Copyright, Designs and Patents Act 1988.

Typeset in Baskerville Regular/Italic &
Narziss Medium Drops by **Ten Storeys®**

Printed in the United Kingdom by Clays Ltd, Elcograf S.p.A.

British Library Cataloguing-in-Publication Data.
A catalogue record for this book is available from the
British Library.

ISBN TBC 978-1-9998960-4-1 (Paperback edition)
ISBN TBC 978-1-9998960-5-8 (Electronic edition)

Some stories first appeared in a different format and
under different titles in the following publications: The
Lady in the Garden in *The Honest Ulsterman;* Sam Watson
& the Penny World Cup, Ultreia and Peas in *The Lonely
Crowd;* The Cowboy in *Long Story Short;* She Will Be My
Joy in *The Penny Dreadful.*

In Memory & Dedicated to:

Vera Guiney

Part One

Part Two

Part Three

Part One

We Knew You Before You Were Born

It was spring when we took you to the Aran Islands. I suppose that was your first real trip. We had signed up for a twelve kilometre run and taken the ferry from the mainland.

Stone walls herded us through the barren landscape of *Inishmaan* and even for a spring day, it was stifling. Roads and tracks undulated. Our views did too. Sometimes we ran towards a broad blue sky, sometimes for the green expanse of the sea. I thought about you as I passed the school and then circled towards the grassy airstrip. It was rewarding in a way, knowing you were there, inside your mum's belly.

Your heart was already beating by then. Quiet as a blade of grass shifting in a breeze. It amazes me to think how our hearts haven't stopped beating since before we were born. No technology can replicate that. This is the wonder of life.

Do you know, you are the only person to have heard mum's heartbeat from the *inside.*?

A right turn took us through a dune and down onto the beach where we tried to stay on the harder sand. The wind was stronger. Running more difficult. There are many things I want to teach you about the world and sand is one of them. A grain is so tiny. You will hear people compare it to many things over the course of your life. You can build castles and dig moats to fill with seawater and draw pictures on its surface, but someday I want you to hold a few grains in your hand, then look at them under a microscope. Will you do that?

There was a long and punishing hill near the end and we both had to walk it, but we finished the race and you did too. That night we learned more about the island. A thick power cable on the seabed provides electricity and is the only physical connection to the mainland. It's umbilical cord. Not long ago they had no power for a month because it was so difficult to access. To repair.

The following morning, we went outside for some air and stopped by a small field. A ewe stood licking a lamb. Another lay still on the grass. Your mum ran inside to tell the owner, who was preparing breakfast.

'Martin, one of the sheep has just given birth.'

'I know,' he said, sausages hissing in the pan. 'I pulled them twenty minutes ago.'

'One of them isn't moving.'

'He will be grand.' He smiled.

A few weeks later we visited your grandparents and asked them each to hold out a hand. Close their eyes. We placed a hazelnut in their palms and watched their puzzled reaction.

'This is the size of your new grandchild.'

Smiles. Hugs. Joy.

As you grew into a plum, then an apple and then a grapefruit, we talked about what life might be like when you came. Would you love raindrops on your face? Adore animals? Whose eyes might you have? We looked forward to taking you into the mountains, to their perfect silence.

We had a small white cat at that time. His name was Edmund. He took to perching himself up on your mother's belly and purring with his head on his front paws. The more it happened, the more we realised there was something protective about the way he liked to come and watch over you.

By the time you were the size of a honeydew melon we knew some of your routine and would talk to you inside your mother's belly just after ten o'clock every night when you woke from your nap and started to move. I thought about you growing in there. Floating in amniotic fluid like a little astronaut.

You kicked a lot. Responded to our voices. You were alert from early on.

'How's our baby?' I'd say.

'Sleeping.' Mum would say. Then other times. 'Wide

awake. Kicking. Turning.'

We found out you were a girl at the second scan. Then you felt even *more* real.

Twenty weeks old. Our daughter. We picked your name. Courageous and kind. Curious explorer of the world.

Scout.

There was a thick and cold fog the night we headed to the hospital with your mum in labour. It was difficult to see. Car lights reflecting off the mist. I drove those treacherous roads and tried to rush, but be sensible at the same time. It was below freezing, minus four. We arrived at the hospital and I had to drop your mother at the doors, to wait alone while I hurried to park the car. I sprinted through the night to help her in. I'll never forget those moments. The cold. That panic.

Night birthed its morning. Followed by a long and tiresome day. Eventually, at 7.36pm, they pulled you from mum's belly and you grabbed onto a gauze on your way out. Took your first real breaths. We heard your voice. Your cries. The surgical team laughed. You would not let go of their gauze. They'd never seen such determination.

When they cleaned and brought you to us, you were wrapped up tight and wore a woollen hat knitted by a retired midwife who couldn't let go of her babies. It had yellow and red stripes, like something Bob Marley would wear. They laughed some more. Somehow it suited your personality, even though they'd only known you for a minute.

But we knew you before you were born. Felt this powerful connection from our hearts to yours, like an invisible spindle of silk. Woven from adoration. Yearning. A need to shelter. It only intensified when we saw your dark eyes. Your perfect nose.

In the recovery ward, you sat in mum's arms with a drip already in your wrist, wrapped in a bandage that made your hand look like a boxing glove.

People couldn't get over how alert you were. Just born. Eyes open.

They kept you both in for a week. Dads were sent home every night at ten and mum would stare at you in the crib. Sometimes she'd lift you and stand by the window to show you the world. Look out across the darkness where the fog still held strong and ghostly lights all had a halo. Ambulances would come and go. Bringing end to a life or one to be repaired. Then there were all those babies. The endless cycle of new life. Raw. Primal. Souls coming and going, circling that hospital building.

In the mornings, I brought coffee and apple cake and spent the day learning how to look after you. How to be your Dad.

After five days the chance of infection had passed and they removed the boxing glove. We loved seeing that little hand for the first time. Another part of you to love. We brought you home, turned the heat on and put you into your Moses basket. The darts was on television. You slept a while. Mum did too.

That first night was long, but only because babies don't know the difference between night and day. You were awake until 5am, so we all sat together on the bed and spent our first night as a family watching whatever film happened to be on the television in those early hours. Your first ever movie was *Kickboxer* starring *Jean-Claude Van Damme*.

Cards came. Visitors did too. People wanted to hold you. Smell your skin.

And today. You turn one year old. Can walk a few steps. Laugh. Say mama and dada. You have taken to hugging things that you like. The cat. A spoon. Dad's shoe.

You get excited when you see bananas. They are your favourite.

One morning you unexpectedly said *Mumbai*.

You have mum's blue eyes, her dimples too, and can make a heart glad with just a smile. You climb stairs with the same determination that grabbed onto that gauze in the hospital and we can do nothing only grin and follow along behind with guiding hands.

People know you are twelve months old, but it has been much longer, for we knew you before you were born.

Summer Stones

By a clear stream, that turns and gently massages over rocks of no importance, hunkers a young girl of six years old. She is a well-behaved, spirited girl who smiles broadly, showing tiny dimples in her cheeks that are so precious, they produce a grin from whoever sees them. Her chestnut hair waves down her back. Already tatty. But she will smooth it as she does every night, with a hundred strokes of the brush. She is humming a hymn that sometimes drifts into song then back to melody again.

There is no real bank to the river. It sneaks across fields, twisting quietly through tall grass and minding its own business. There are particular places where cows like to stop for a drink and the grass is worn, leaving a makeshift muddy shore. It is during warmer months that the girl sometimes removes her shoes and socks. Walks across the dried mud and into the shallows where the currents tickle her toes and sticklebacks dart. This particular field has hedged borders and from the river sweeps up into a long sprawl of lush meadow where the cattle prefer to graze. A big oak tree shelters them from rain. Or sometimes they stand by a single metal gate to watch the goings on. Jaws chewing side to side. In the concrete street known locally as *the hill,* sits a row of houses. The girl lives in number six. Same as her age.

In her hands she holds small stones. Each one in turn is washed in the stream then examined at great length. Most are tossed into thorns and brambles. Into the river itself. Depending on which thoughts fire in her brain first. The odd time, she will stand, pull back, and throw the pebble as far as she can out into the meadow, then hunker again as though it never happened.

Sometimes, after careful consideration, she finds a stone with a quality she likes. She will smile and place it into her trough. There are many stones inside. All of them angel white or speckled with silver. Gold. Some so perfectly shaped she knows they were fashioned by the hand of God himself.

This is the fortieth day of summer and she has been selecting stones every day.

The first one is still the most special. She had been down by the river, feeding her two favourite cows who she recognised by yellow tags on their ears. Numbers thirty-three and eighty-seven. She pulled out clumps of grass and held her palm flat, for that is the way you handfeed cows. Horses too. And donkeys. As she washed her hands in the water, then watched sunshine glint off her dripping fingers, she had spied the sparkle of a bright object and reached into the stream. A white stone. Perfectly smooth. Like something from heaven. It had mesmerised her, that first one. Into her pocket. Out again. Examine. The most beautiful stone she had ever seen. She had wondered where it came from. How it got there. Did not take long until she began searching for more. Perhaps the river held other pretty stones?

By the end of that first day, she had carried five home in the pockets of her dress. Lined them up on the front door step.

Beautiful white.

Grey speckled.

A reddish one. Shaped like a banana.

A dull white with gold spots.

A smooth grey, in the shape of Pacman.

On the second day she had seen something in the river, like a model boat that had sunk and listed to one side. As she approached, it felt like something that needed to be rescued. She pulled it onto the grass. Turned it over. There was still mud caked into the corners and she recognised it as a window box that sits on sills like Mrs. McEldane's in number seven who always has beautiful flowers that are bright and bulge and dangle down over the rim.

She smiled. It was not from the hill, so she did not have to return it to anyone. It was a gift that has sailed to her. A container to keep her treasure safe. She appreciates the things people find of little value.

From then on she spent every day at the river's edge seeking the most perfect of stones and pebbles to fill the window box. Only beautiful ones of every sculpt and nuance nature could make.

It would be the most special thing she'd ever done.

Each day she dragged the box up home through soft meadow grass, wearing trails like the grooves of her grandmother's hands. Her parents remarked on the beautiful stones just to keep her entertained.

Now, after many days of sift and select, the trough is nearing two thirds full. She has borrowed a cart to ferry it up and down the hill, for she can barely lift it anymore.

When evenings come, she leaves the trough in her back yard and hopes everything will be as it was when she wakes the following morning.

A shed would be ideal, but they do not own one.

She worries about the boy in number three. He has a couple of years on her and already a reputation for stealing things. The day he came across her wheeling the trough home, she explained it with lacklustre and emphasised only girls would be interested.

So far, the trough hasn't been stolen.

The sun is high and bright, pinching the blue of her eyes as she pulls. She is halfway up the hill, stopping for a rest. Sometimes she wants to sit on the wall that follows the road. But is forbidden. There is a fierce river down the other side and the drop is steep and dangerous.

How special her stones look. When the trough is full, she might ask for some paint from her grandpa or a neighbour to clean it up. Yesterday a bee landed in the stones to investigate and she watched him briefly, before shooing him away.

She knows all bees are boys.

Just today, a yellow butterfly flickered through the still wildflowers down in the meadow, before meandering into the trough. She tried to steal a pebble and the girl shooed her too.

She knows that all butterflies are girls.

As the girl rests and mulls about a drink she might like to have, the chug of a car ascending the hill draws her gaze. It passes. Stops. Reverses a little.

She knows who it is. There are few cars on the hill and she can recognise each by their sound alone. Her grandpa steps out of his brown car. It is old, but shiny and clean. He walks slowly. Plods. That is just his way. His hair is waxed grey and catches the sun, his face in half smile.

'What have you got there?' he asks.

'My stones. Wanna see?'

He looks into the trough and wipes his brow. 'Where did you get all this?'

'Down at the stream, I'm collecting nice ones.'

'You shouldn't be anywhere near the river.'

He pulls a white handkerchief from his pocket. Rubs his nose. Bends to lift the trough. Hauls it up to his shoulder.

The dimpled smile slips from her face as he turns it over the wall. Stones and pebbles tumble in a kaleidoscopic avalanche to the river below. He drops the trough at her feet. A grey stone with speckles of silver rattles to a halt. She recognises it from the first day. He takes it in his fingertips and tosses it over the wall.

He is soon home on the hill, brewing tea and eating apple tart. She sits by the road with an empty cart. Lip shaking. Quiet.

In the days that follow she will retrieve the trough and climb over the wall where she is forbidden to go, but most of the stones will be gone. She will try to recreate her perfection, but summer will soon be gone too.

Peas

A fire burns in the hearth, its lazy glow flickering upon the walls, its crackle-hum drifting into the hall and down towards the kitchen. There at the table, a boy is hunched over a sheet of paper. The writing is neat to him but messy to anyone else, for he has taken into the joins of his letters with too much gusto and too much slant. He sets down his pencil and bends the paper into a fold, then walks across in his red slippers and chequered robe to the kitchen counter. The oven drones in repetitive timbres and the smell of roasting turkey savours the air with a taste of anticipation.

Reaching for a high cupboard, he tries tiptoes first, then climbs onto the bench so he can open it properly. He sets out a small white plate and a tall glass with yellow flowers painted up the side. Climbs down to a low cupboard. Finds a bottle of orange squash. He pours an inch into the glass, then fills it up with water at the sink until the yellow petals are submerged.

He places his folded note on the plate, then slides the glass of juice in beside it and steps back to look at the arrangement like a photographer arranging a shot. A bowl filled with water and steeping peas is in the way and he pushes it aside.

The boy goes to the other side of the cooker near the tall fridge, where there is a pyramid of chocolate crisped buns, each in a blue-striped papery cradle. He lifts two. Brings them to his plate. He would like one of them himself but is not allowed another, so instead, carefully breaks a small chunk from the bottom of each and munches it down.

'What're you at?' asks an older brother.

The boy hasn't heard him come in. He takes a piece of shortbread from a round tin and places it on the plate. 'Getting the stuff ready to leave out for Santa.'

The brother unfolds the note. Nods with approval. 'Very good. You're spoiling Santa rotten! Juice and everything!' His eyes are suddenly alight. He puts his fingertips into the bowl of soaking peas. Takes one out. Lifts a bun out of its paper and hides a pea underneath. He laughs.

'You can't do that,' says the boy.

The brother puts a pea under the other bun, sniggers, then drops two peas into the glass of juice.

'I hope you two aren't eating all those buns?' says the

mother. The boy hasn't heard her come in either.

'No, we're just leaving this stuff out for Santa.' He rearranges the items on the plate. Makes himself look busy. By the time he looks again, she is beside him and he hears his brother clumping up the stairs.

She touches his shoulder. Reads the note and places it back on the plate. 'That's a great wee note. Santa will love it, and two buns?' She smiles. Rubs his back. 'Away you go and leave it on the hearth.'

She turns off the oven and opens it up. Turkey steam rises to meet the ceiling.

The boy carries his juice and food to the living room where the walls illuminate in soft firelight. At one end of the mantelpiece hangs two black socks. For the parents. At the other end are three. Different colour for each brother. Grey, black, white. The father is lying up the sofa half-asleep, watching a black and white film on the television. The boy places the treats and his note on the warm fire tiles, then stands a moment to catch the film. An old man is sitting by an open fire supping soup in his pyjamas and wearing a limp hat. His eyebrows are bushy. He is sharp-faced. The father holds out a long box of after-eights. The boy takes one and eats it. Now there is rattling. A sound like chains. The old man stops mid-slurp to listen. Turns. Another man appears. See-through, like a ghost. The old man in the drooping hat becomes frightened. It is a little scary so the boy looks away. He sees the snow globe on the mantel. Washing lines of cards, slung from wall to wall. The red and blue and green lights of the Christmas tree are steady, then twinkling, then steady again.

'Is that you ready?' says the father.

'Ready to rock and roll. Night, night.'

'Night, night.'

The boy goes into the hall and along to the kitchen doorway. His mother has the turkey out on the bench and covered with silvery foil.

'Night, Night.' He calls in.

'Is that you all set?' she says, closing a drawer.

'Yes.'

'Night, night, see you in the morning. Hope he comes.'

He smiles. She does too.

As he climbs the stairs he doesn't mind that it is dark, for tonight he doesn't need the light. The fifth step creaks as always, then he is at the top, pausing outside his brothers' room to listen to the film he is not allowed to watch. He hears a gunshot. The sound of a car screeching. One of the brothers laughs. They are talking now. He leans closer to the door. Tries to focus on their voices.

'Santa Claus won't be coming to him!' one of them says. They both laugh. Dramatic music. More gunshots.

The boy turns into his own room where moonlight illuminates the carpet in dull silver. He decides to leave the curtains open, to be ready for a glimpse of the man in the big red suit, then wonders who his brother was referring to. *Who* won't Santa be coming to? He closes the door and shuffles off his slippers. Climbs into bed. They better not have been talking about him, for he took nothing to do with the peas in the juice. He hopes that Santa will see the funny side of it. Won't choke on them. As he pulls the duvet up to his ear, he knows it will be a long night of shifting and turning and straining to hear sleigh bells. He hopes for snow and the things he has asked for, though has been sure not to ask for too much. He knows when the televisions are off and the house falls into silence, eventually some things become certain.

He will wake. It will be morning. First, he will listen for sounds of movement in the house. A creaking door. Low cough. Someone running a tap. He will dress quickly and look out for snow. The family will gather on the landing. Talk about whether or not Santa made it. As he descends the stairs there will always be an inkling of doubt, but then, as he rounds the corner and enters the cool living room, with embers spent in the hearth, the excitement will flood inside him and he will wonder why he wavered at all, because no matter what, he comes, Santa always comes.

Plenty of Salt

I arrive at the yard. It is already warm. Another day of drinking straight from the hose to cool down. The lorry is there as normal with its tailgate lowered and I see the boss, but no sign of Gordon the delivery man who is as wide as a house.

'You.' He points at me. 'Come over here. Drop your stuff off. You're coming with me to help with the deliveries.'

'Where's Gordon?'

'He's sick.'

I am hopeful I have been chosen for my hard work ethic, that he has noticed me these past weeks from afar, and not just because I am the first to show up this morning. He closes up the tailgate. Secures the doors.

'Right. Let's go. What's your name again?'

'Richie.'

THE GIFT HOUSE
C.I.F. 25715690-B
DARSENA DE LEVANTE
LOCAL B-29
29630 BENALMADENA
MALAGA

NFra. simplificada 0-00023369
Fecha : 31/10/2019 Hora 10:50
Vendedor: Vendedor por defecto

Descripcion	Cant	P.V.P	Total
CALENDARIOS GR.	1	11,95	11,95

Tipo	Base	Iva	SubTotal
21	9,88	2,07	11,95

Total   11,95 €

Cobro por   Caja Euros   20,00

Total Cobrado   20,00
Thanks for your visit.05

He climbs in and before I even have time to think about any of it, we are on the road. I've never been in a lorry, so part of me is excited to sit up high. See over hedges. Out across the fields. I am nervous but try to be enthusiastic.

'So, where are we headed Mr. Harrison?'

'Coleraine direction.'

'Is this lorry petrol or diesel?'

'Diesel.'

'Did you see the match last night?'

This is where he sighs and chooses not to speak for the rest of the two hour journey.

The sky is as blue as I've ever seen it. Sun blinding. Sometimes I close my eyes for a moment. Harrison pulls down his sun-visor. I do the same. Among the grind and shift of gears, he grunts the odd time. The radio is on, but low, and this intermittent fuzz scrapes through the country music like a persistent clawing animal. I glance to try and catch the details of his face, for our interactions have always been fleeting. Him walking past me in one of the poly-tunnels, or driving in and out of the yard in his Black Mercedes. He has dark eyes. Heavy jowls. Hair slicked back with oil. Along with all of the other creases in his skin, Harrison looks stern. He is hard to like.

I look out the window and wonder what has happened to big fat Gordon. Some of the boys at the yard played a joke on him last week. He had parked up the lorry in the afternoon and left the tailgate down, then went into the Garden Centre for a cup of tea. When he returned, I heard him shouting,

'Yis wee bastards! Yis absolute wee bastards!'

Of course, anyone who was around the yard at the time came to see what the fuss was about. Someone had found an enormous pair of grey Y-Fronts in the lorry and laid them out flat on the tailgate like an elephant's ear. I don't know why they were in the lorry in the first place, but it was a laugh.

Harrison presses a button. Lowers both our windows. Rests an elbow on the doorframe and I do the same. The rushing air is warm, but refreshing in its own way. I cannot help but think about my older brothers taunting me about Harrison. They have done since I found myself this summer job. Although they will never actually explain things in detail, one thing is certain, it sounds like a bad idea to be left alone with him. Something had happened a few years ago up the big back field to a young boy worker - *very much like you* - the brothers would say, then snigger. They also laugh at every mention of his name, so there is *something* in the story.

Harrison puts on the *tick-ah, tick-ah, tick-ah* of the indicator and the lorry begins to slow. I watch him wrestle the wide steering wheel. Fight against the coughing engine. We shunt the kerb once, then twice. He kills the ignition. The cab is quiet except for a long whining beep that eventually cuts to silence. I expect him to show concern, for us to jump out and wrench open the massive blue doors, stand hands on hips and shake our heads at the mess. I picture flower baskets swinging wildly. Petals floating like feathers in a disturbed chicken coop.

I even know how to open the tailgate. Pull the lever in the direction to go. Press the green button. The lorry will need to be unloaded, flowers and shrubs delivered, money handed over.

Harrison pulls out a tatty tenner that looks like it has been planted, failed to grow into a money tree, and then dug up again.

'Away over to that chip-shop and get me a chip,' he says, squinting. 'I want plenty of salt now. Make sure you ask for plenty of salt.'

'Just salt?'

'*Plenty* of salt.'

I open the door. It creaks. I think about my sandwiches back at the yard. It could be hours before we get home. Maybe the other boys will eat my lunch.

'And get yourself something.' Harrison scowls. 'And make sure you bring the change.'

I climb out. For adults it is one step or two, for me a climb.

'And ask for a receipt!'

The door offers a tinny, unkind clunk. I wander towards the back of the lorry. Want to open the doors and check everything is alright, but the chip-shop is right across the road. While I wait for cars to pass, all I can think of is salt, salt, plenty of salt. *And bring a receipt.*

I burst across the road at full pelt to try and impress him. A woman wearing a blue apron and matching hat is battling against some bird shit on the window. She smears it into a dirty white circle.

I go inside. The woman follows. Goes behind the counter. 'What'll it be, love?'

My standard order for chip-shops is a hamburger with ketchup. It's what I like and is cheap enough to suit my pocket. But Harrison might kill me for ordering a hamburger. I look up at the menu. Scan the prices.

Hamburger - ninety-five pence.

Chips - sixty pence.

For a moment, I consider going for it. But know Harrison will pin me to a post in one of his fields. Turn me into a scarecrow.

'Just two chips please. One with salt and vinegar. The other with *just* salt. *Plenty* of salt.'

I worry about getting the order right. About Harrison. People can push a rumour to the depths of their brain, but it still exists. Lurking. Playing like a distant record. My brothers call him *The Flasher*. I don't even know what that is. Something dirty I think.

'No problem, love. That'll be a few minutes.'

And I don't even like chips. As I listen to the fryer sizzle, I suddenly have a thought and scarper outside, waiting by the kerb for a gap to cross. Harrison stares. I run as fast as I can to the lorry. He looks down with his best *what-the-hell-do-you-think-you're-doing* face on.

'Do you want anything to drink?'

'No. Just a chip with plenty of salt, isn't that what I told you?'

'Alright.'

I run back across. I'm taking too much time now. Harrison will probably dock my pay for time wasting. Take the chips out of my wages too.

The woman shovels them out. Smiles. I watch her intently as she shakes salt over both. Sprays the vinegar over mine. Then I am sure I experience that thing grownups sometimes talk about. A heart attack.

I wave my hands. *'No vinegar on that one!'*

She sets it down without pouring a drop. Glares at me. 'I know, love.'

I pay with the ragged tenner and calculate the change to verify what she gives me is correct. She hands over the wrapped chips. The money in my palm reminds me of Harrison's wife. She pays the wages on Fridays. Is nice to all the workers. I'm glad Harrison doesn't do the pay or every tenner would be filthy and crumpled. I wonder if she knows her husband is a flasher?

At the door, I see him across the road. Staring. Turned right around in his seat to face the chip-shop. The woman comes back out to finish wiping off her bird shit.

'Sorry missus, can I have a receipt?'

'We don't do receipts love, sorry.'

Harrison is going to murder and bury me out in the big field that took all summer to grow his Sweet William.

No-one will ever know. I hesitate at the kerb. First time asking for a receipt in my life. Didn't go well. Maybe I should have argued with her? Demanded she write one out?

I hold a bag of chips in each hand and turn my concentration up full.

His on the left. Mine on the right.

I am at the lorry door like a bullet.

His on the left. Mine on the right.

'What took you so long?'

'It was just yer woman there. She was too busy cleaning the windows.'

Although Harrison is turned towards the chip-shop now and has his back to me, I know he is firing dirty looks at the woman across the road. I hand over the change and a parcel of chips.

'Did you get a receipt?'

'She said they don't do receipts.'

'Well how much is two chips?'

'One pound twenty.'

He counts the change. Puts it into his trouser pocket. Looks from the corner of his eye at me. He opens his chips and they fill the cab with a salty steam that softens his face a little. He stuffs them into his angry mouth and says nothing. He seems almost happy.

I struggle to eat mine. Don't even have anything to drink. I am too scared to speak. I leave a few in the wrapper and scrunch them up quickly so that he doesn't notice. Then, even though I am dying of thirst, I thank Harrison for the food.

He clears his throat. Starts the engine. 'Thon was some second goal last night.'

His head is already out the window. We pull into the road. I have to acknowledge him because, right enough, the goal was good.

'Was indeed. An absolute screamer.'

Sam Watson &
The Penny World Cup

Let me tell you about how we used to gallivant, my cousins and I, back when we were boys. Saturdays would begin with Bap, Vince, Gunter and myself (Goin) all squeezed around their kitchen table pulling apart slices of bread and placing them carefully into bowls of hot tomato soup. Mostly, we'd push a spoon through this flotsam until it became tomatoey mush, but on occasion one of us came up with a new idea that always turned out to be bad. It would be something ridiculous like crumbling a chocolate biscuit over the top or adding mustard - though we all knew that nothing worked as well as the traditional mush and it was always enjoyable to watch a new idea go wrong.

There was a fellow who lived eight doors down, a man-mountain at age eleven called McGrath, who we were surprised to discover also had his Saturday tomato soup ritual. McGrath claimed he would sprinkle grated cheese into the saucepan just as the soup was beginning to boil. What a weirdo! We all knew you couldn't improve on the perfection of Heinz Tomato Soup and had no desire to taste such a ridiculous concoction, but Bap once saw him make it as described, so it certainly wasn't a fairy-tale. I guess adding half a block of cheese to every bowl of soup helped explain his size. McGrath was a man-boy who could grow a goatee on command. Even at eleven years old.

Anyway, after the soup we scrubbed to get rid of our orange moustaches and Gunter, the youngest (God love him), didn't know any better so kept his. Then it was time to visit Watson's sweet shop and that is what I want to talk to you about. You see, Watsons was one of those poky little shops that was a bit like a supermarket crammed into a shoe box. Shelves everywhere. Laddered up to the ceiling. You could say it had an identity problem and I think the owner would have sold anything if he thought it might bring in a profit. You could rent videos. Buy detergent. Shelves behind the counter were cluttered with stationery, nuts and bolts, fuses, lightbulbs, rolls of flypaper, magic trees for your car, toilet roll. There were canned goods and bottles of fizzy pop with Middle Eastern writing on the back. The coke for instance, didn't taste the same.

Sometimes there'd be a batch of toasters. Handsaws. Toilet seats with a barbed wire design. There were

toothbrushes. Hairbrushes. Men's ties. Thermos Flasks.
If you needed an ointment or cream, Watsons would
have it. Basically it was the place to go if you needed
anything at all, but we were only interested in the sweets.

From the outside, it looked like someone had one day
decided to turn their house into a shop. The windows
were covered in old adverts. Wall's Ice-Cream, featuring
kids with sixties hairdos. A faded poster advertising
'Squeak' Mousetraps with a cartoon image of a dazed
mouse clamped at its neck. There were cobwebs. Pieces
of old Sellotape scattered across the glass. A neon Coke
sign that was never lit. Watson's allowed the locals to put
up items too, so there was a cat that had been missing
for four years. An ironing board for sale. An invite to
last year's kids Christmas Party in the community centre.
There wasn't much effort put into window dressing, you
get the drift.

Once you went inside, it was like an old person had
once lived there and left behind their musty carpet
and stippled, dirty-cream wallpaper. The guy behind
the counter was called Sam, he was cool, and we all
automatically presumed he was the owner, so we referred
to him as *Sam Watson*. It turned out years later he was
actually called Sam McCall and just worked there, but to
us he was Sam Watson and he owned the place.

So Sam was this hip, mid-thirties guy with long dark
hair – I guess it was a mullet – who made it appear like he
was just sitting there every Saturday, waiting specifically

on us to come in through the door. I don't know how he did it, maybe it was in his smile, but he should have been a hotel concierge or perhaps even a movie star.

Sam would stand up from his stool and we would stampede the counter, for whoever got there first got most of the conversation.

'How's it goin', fellas?
'Are yis lookin' forward to the football matches today?'
'Are yis headin' up the town?'
'Did yis see Liverpool last night. God, they were awful.'

There was an eagerness to him and he was an exceptional listener. But the sweet counter was the only thing in the shop that seemed organised. Plastic tubs of penny sweets were lined right along the top and underneath the glass in neat rows. He really did have quite the selection. Sam would talk us through what was selling well, what was new in that week and what his personal favourites were. Then he would lick his thumb and forefinger, snag a white paper bag from the pile, and deal with whoever was first.

It is at this point I will digress to tell you about a greengrocer nearby who also sold sweets. After you passed through a tunnel of carrots and broccoli and other veg piled high to the roof, tucked away in at the back were shelves of those grand sweet tubs, you know, the ones that get measured out in quarters? Sherbet strawberries. Lemon bonbons. Midget gems. To be honest, his sweets were the best in town, but there were reasons why we connoisseurs didn't go there. Firstly, he had a stupid sign on his door, which read:

'Only two boys allowed at a time'.

To be fair, a naïve person might think, *oh, it's because his shop is long and narrow. There isn't the room. What else could he do only put that sign up?* But you could soon go inside and find ten old ladies mulling about and stuffing fruit into their brown paper bags! It was discrimination is what it was! The way he smiled was annoying too. More like a dog showing its teeth. He refused to allow notices on his windows and as if all of that wasn't enough, the clincher was this. Mucky hands. He'd move from handling dirty turnips, to sticking his bare, grimy hands into the sweet tub. His bare hands!

So Watson's was our chosen establishment. No contest.

Although we were eager to talk to Sam, there was never a fight over who was first to buy their sweets. We needed time to assess and plan. Peer through the glass. Maybe there were new ones Sam had forgotten to tell us about. So someone ordered ten of something, five of something else, and how much are they Sam? And Sam patiently counted out each penny sweet into your sweetie bag. Let me tell you, if you asked Sam for forty red laces and twenty green laces, he would stand there and count them out for you individually like he was counting gold bullion. At times, we would linger in Watsons for a good thirty minutes and he never groaned, complained or rushed.

After Watson's, we usually went to the football pitches up at the school for a kick around. Ate our sweets on the way. If it was a crappy day, we'd head up the town and check out the toy shop, the sports shop and sometimes detour down to the swimming pool to sit in the spectator area and keep out of the rain. We'd munch sweets, but try to keep some for watching the football match on the television later that afternoon.

The town was small, so there were two things we had to be vigilant for at all times:

• The Bad Man
• The Cuzzies.

The Bad Man always wore black. Had black hair and a black moustache. He looked creepy enough to avoid on looks alone, but there had been something years ago involving him and a child and our parents all warned us to stay away from him.

The Cuzzies were bigger boys that always wanted to beat up my cousins and anyone they hung around with, which also meant me.

If we saw The Cuzzies, we ran like hell. If we saw The Bad Man, we kept a safe distance.

Now you know how we spent our Saturdays gallivanting, I want to tell you about this one day in particular when we walked into Watson's shop and there was Sam Watson, the owner who wasn't really the owner, and whose name wasn't really Watson, but McCall, sitting behind the counter. Ready for us.

'How are you today, fellas?' He bounced off his stool. Clapped his hands together. 'Let me tell you about this competition I'm runnin' over the next couple of weeks. I came up with this idea, what with the footy World Cup comin' up soon, that I'd run a competition for all the kids who come in and buy the sweets. It's called the Penny World Cup.'

Sam came out from behind the counter. It was only then that we noticed the Coca-Cola watch hung on the wall. And when I say watch, what I mean is, just think of a normal sized clock hung on your wall, now imagine someone adding red straps that are a few feet long and writing Coca-Cola in the nicest script you have ever seen, then *voila*, you have a massive Coca-Cola watch.

To be honest with you, we thought it was pretty rubbish. We must have been ten years old at the time and it was something that a pre-eight year old would have found impressive. It had a cheap, plastic look about it and it was the only ever time, that Sam didn't quite have his finger on the pulse of children's needs.

'What it is fellas,' continued Sam, 'I'm runnin' this Penny World Cup to coincide with the real Italia '90 World Cup and the way it works is, say…you buy twenty cola bottles…then your name goes on the chart here with twenty written beside it. Then if nobody else beats that by the closin' date, you win the big watch.'

He waited for our excitement. None came. We stared blankly and his eyes lost some of their sparkle.

'The second prize is a crazy pair of Coca-Cola sunglasses that are so wide, they stick out the side of your face! They're pretty cool as well.'

I think we all felt a little sorry for him in that moment. The whole thing sounded like a load of crap.

'That sounds good, Sam,' said Vince. We turned to look at him. Had he had gone mad in the head? There was the slightest hint of a joke in his expression that only people who knew him well could detect. We knew what he was doing. Offering Sam encouragement.

Bap followed his lead. 'What if you buy, let's say, fifty blackjacks, is that no good?'

'Yes! That means you would go into the lead on the chart with fifty. It doesn't matter what you buy, whoever spends the most pennies, will win. That's why it's called the Penny World Cup.' Sam's entusiasm levels went up again. 'You can't mix though. So if you bought fifty fruity frogs and forty white mice, then you'd only go on the chart for the fifty fruities.'

I asked when the closing date was and Sam said two weeks, just before the actual World Cup starts.

'Bap put 50p on the counter. 'Give me fifty blackjacks!'

'Great job, Bap! That's you top of the leader-board.' He counted them out, then wrote Bap's name.

Sam was smiling, buzzing even.

Now there isn't a lot to be said for buying a bag of sweets that are all the same, because part of the enjoyment is the variety and *choosing* the variety, but we were caught in the competition of it now and as a bonus would be humouring Sam.

We all rifled our pockets, counted our coins.

'I'll have sixty-five red laces!' Vince went top.

'Give me seventy-one fizzbombs!' I was the leader.

'Seventy-two cola bottles!' Gunter went top.

I can't deny that it gave us a kick trying to better each other and it was rewarding in a strange way to have seen Sam so happy. We went to the football pitches afterwards and played *Headers and Volleys* for a while, before going home to finish our sweets and watch football on the television. The following week would be even more exciting, going back to Watsons to see who was winning the Penny World Cup. None of us were fussed on the giant watch, and even though they seemed rubbish at first, we all now had our eyes on those crazy Coca-Cola sunglasses.

By the time the following Saturday came around and we had already finished our mushy tomato soup, each of us had secretly in our heads, planned out a strategy for how to win the Penny World Cup. Our pocket money amounted to £1.50 each, so there was only so much to work with.

We made our way down towards Watsons to find the strangest thing we had ever laid eyes on. A queue. Coming right out the door!

'Look at this carry on!' said Gunter.

'Is this all for the Penny World Cup?' said Bap.

Vince stopped. Turned. Started walking away. 'There's the Cuzzies...there's the friggin' Cuzzies!'

We all turned. Glanced back.

They had already seen us. Started to chase. We ran and followed Vince. Adrenalin powering us forward. He broke right after the end house and cut through wasteland.

'What are we gonna do?' said Gunter. He was the youngest. I could see the panic in his face.

'Head for the building site,' said Vince. 'Grab some stones. Arm yourselves!'

More than anything, I remember this as the day we came so close to having the shit beaten out of us, but here is what happened next.

The Cuzzies. Three of them. Big lads. Looked sixteen or seventeen to me. Came across the wasteland and we began to pelt them with stones. Stones that were so tiny they were pathetic. We might as well have been throwing bubbles at them. But everything missed or fell short.

They just laughed. Clenched their fists and kept coming.

I could see the bravery forming in Vince's face. Jaw hardening. Eyes focused. He was the oldest and therefore the one with responsibility for protecting us. They would attack him first. Then us.

I lifted a rock the size of an apple. Pulled back my arm and threw it so hard that I stumbled forward and landed chest on the ground. All the air slapped out of my lungs. They would not inflate again. I got up and stood hunched over, trying to breathe.

'You got him, Goin! Such a shot!'

I drew a thimble of breath. Made a strange noise, like a donkey.

Vince patted my back. 'You alright? You got him.'

I winced. Could barely get a word out. 'Winded.'

By the time I could breathe properly again, the Cuzzies were gone. Everyone was elated.

'Such a throw! You split one of their heads open. The blood ran down his face!'

'You wanna seen him runnin' off. Cryin' his eyes out.'

'The fear on their faces when it happened.'

'They'll think twice before chasin' us again.'

I felt like I was going to get in trouble, but no one else seemed worried so I tried not to panic about it either. We went back to Watsons, intending to go straight to the chart on the wall and see who was winning, but believe me when I tell you, we were alarmed at the sight we saw. There was no longer a queue, but the shop was chaotic. Sam was so engrossed in dealing with other boys, he didn't even see us come in. He was laughing, eyes alight as he counted out sweets into bags and wrote a new name on the leader board. We managed to catch a glimpse. The current leader had bought three hundred and twenty-two fizzbombs. Our names had sunk to the bottom like stones tossed into a river.

We looked at each other. Felt uncomfortable. And

there was even Dessie Donaldson, the thieving little bollocks, mooching about. He went to our school. Would steal anything he could get his hands on. Pens. Rulers. Even stole someone's skateboard from their garden and painted it with emulsion to disguise the deed! I didn't really know what it meant at the time, but more and more we'd hear adults say about Dessie – *he'd steal the eye out of your head and then come back to shit in the hole!*

Everything was wrong, but just wait until you hear this! We got close enough to the front to witness hundreds of fried eggs being loaded into white bags for this bespectacled fellow we did not know. We waited to see what the total would be. Just as Sam added his name – John Greer – to the chart for four hundred fried eggs, and the bespectacled fellow stood smiling, another boy with weird hair and a wonky eye declared that he wanted six hundred jelly turtles! Do you know when a dog gets so excited, that it surpasses tail-wagging and its entire body begins to shake? That was Sam. He kept saying, 'Brilliant! Brilliant!' and shaking his head in disbelief as he scribbled new totals onto the chart. The young fellow left the shop with so many jelly turtles, they had to be put in a carrier bag. A carrier bag! Then finally, Sam turned his attention to us.

'Did you see that boys? Stevie Carson there, just broke the record. I can't see anyone beatin' that, I think the big watch is goin' to be his.'

We all knew that between us, even with our money

combined, we couldn't beat this Stevie Carson fellow, whoever he was. And who the hell were all these strange faces we'd never seen before? So, we just bought our sweets as normal. A nice variety.

Sam didn't seem interested in us. No mention of football. Didn't ask how we were. All he said was, 'Oh... so you aren't goin' for the Penny World Cup anymore, just back to the usual?'

He was unnerved too, as he counted out our orders. Impatient even. Eventually he said the words that we never thought we would hear, 'I'm sorry lads, goin' to have to rush you along. There's a queue buildin' again for the Penny World Cup.'

That following week when we went in, the Penny World Cup had finished and Hamhawk from my class in school had already won the big watch. We couldn't have cared less what his winning total was – eight pounds thirty worth of green laces - and certainly had no interest in knowing who had won the sunglasses. There were still other boys in the shop, hanging around, talking to Sam. And Dessie Donaldson again. The thief. We didn't like this new clientele and didn't stay long.

The Saturday after that, we couldn't bring ourselves to go in, so went to the big supermarket up the town instead. All glaring lights and shiny floors. You couldn't buy a selection of sweets, only bars of chocolate the size of your own head. Something had definitely changed inside us, but it was difficult to put a finger on what exactly it was. In that one day we avoided Watsons, we saw The Bad Man and the Cuzzies within half an hour of each other. In one day! But the Cuzzies glanced in our direction and walked on.

Rumours began to circulate in school then, that Sam had left Watsons. We talked about it in the playground and agreed to meet at home-time. We would go in. See if it was true.

We didn't speak much on the way there. It was like attending a funeral we did not want to go to. When we went inside, he wasn't there, but then, we didn't know if he worked in Watson's every day or not, so that Saturday, we went back and sure enough, no sign of Sam.

The one rumour we heard the most was *He's away to live in England*, but the day I mentioned that to my mother, her eyes told me it wasn't true even though she said it was.

Something gnawed inside each of us. We needed closure. And we missed him.

'Right, we need to come up with what happened to Sam,' said Vince. 'No matter how many people we've asked, no-one can give us an answer, so why don't we, the four of us, all make up a reason, write it on a bit of paper and put it in a hat. Whatever one we pick out, then that'll be what happened to Sam.'

We liked the idea. Took a few days to think it over, then gathered around the kitchen table and while we ate our tomato soup, each wrote on our paper. We had a cereal bowl to put them in.

'Should we read them out before we put them in the bowl?' said Bap.

'Here, I'll do it.' Vince took our notes.

'What really happened to Sam is...' he opened the note, 'he got signed to play for Man Utd. Star striker.'

We laughed.

He opened the next note. 'What really happened to Sam is...he went to work in the Willy Wonka Chocolate Factory.'

He hadn't got to my note yet. Read the next one. 'What really happened to Sam is...he opened a waxwork museum in London where all the people are made out of sweets!'

'Wait,' said Bap. 'To be honest with yis, I think that Goin should get the final say on what happened to Sam, because he was the one that saved us from the Cuzzies. If he hadn't landed that stone on the Cuzzies head, we would have gotten the crap beaten clean out of us.' He folded his arms. 'That's just what I think.'

'Let's vote on it,' said Gunter. 'Everyone in favour of Goin having the final say, put yer hand up.'

They raised their hands. I followed.

'Right,' said Vince, 'Whatever this last note says is what really happened to Sam and this is what we will always remember when we talk about him. This will be our truth.'

He shook out his arms. 'Give me a drumroll.'

Bap started to tap the table with both hands.

He opened the note. 'What really happened to Sam is…he went to work in America as a fake Santa Claus. Ho! Ho! Ho!'

Everyone smiled.

'Sammy Claus!' said Gunter.

That day as we ate our soup, a relief came over each of us, for now we knew that Sam was alive and well and bringing his smile to kids in America. We would miss him, there was no doubt about that, but he was halfway around the world and doing good work. We felt the sense of an ending then, that that period of our lives was over, but then, we were merely boys who would grow up someday to become men. There would be more of life's eras. Seasons. Some would be individual experiences. Some joint. But no matter how many football seasons passed, how many World Cups, we always had those memories to hold onto.

Sisters

The youngest fancies boys already. She is Emily. Six years old. One of her cousins is handsome, so she has a thing for him, but none of the subtlety to go with it. Amongst the family it is already accepted she may well grow up to be a rock star, for she has that uncontrollable spirit.

Her eyes are brown and bright, her hair a rich fawn and always a tangle of mischief. At age five she got her first hairstyle and cried getting it done. By the end she was beaming at her new bob. Cute. Tomboy turned girl in the hairdresser's chair.

Her sister Olivia is three years older. Blue eyes. She is growing tall and graceful, already elegant, like the most perfect of ponies. She aspires to be a princess and amongst the family it is becoming less of a joke and more of a possibility.

They are in the park behind their home. Allowed

to play within calling distance of their mother. Emily likes to stretch the boundary, Olivia keeps control. It is autumn and they gather acorns under the low-hanging branches that reach down to the grass with their crooked fingertips.

The lake is wide and row-boat season is coming to an end. The girls often stand and watch boats on the bright water, but today there are none and the lake is a slab of dark glass. They are allowed to go close enough, but no nearer than the length of their back garden. Emily likes to gain a foot now and then, pretends she doesn't measure too well. Olivia says she will tell Dad, but says it in a nice way.

Their pockets are stuffed with acorns and they talk about how if they only had a basket, they could gather even more. Emily suggests they go home and get two breakfast bowls, her bright brown eyes filled with the idea, but Olivia says Mum wouldn't allow it.

Emily bolts toward the lake. Olivia calls after. She makes it right to the edge and throws an acorn at a passing swan. She misses. The acorn halts to a float. Olivia pulls her back to the invisible boundary, but does it in a kind way.

The swan pivots to determine whether or not it is being fed. Hisses as Emily fires another acorn.

'That thing'll bite you, Emily.'

'How will it, sure it's in the water.'

'It'll soon come out if you keep throwing things at it.'

Emily is a rock star. She throws another, then another. Her hand is rooting in a pocket for the next one. The swan hisses some more, flaps its wings and before they know it, is on the shore. The older sister grabs the younger's arm and tries taking them to safety, but the younger is moving in the wrong direction. Towards the swan.

Massive wings open like a water angel.

Now they both squeal and run.

They almost manage to get away, but Emily is pecked on the leg. It is enough to start her tears. As they go, holding hands, running and weeping, acorns fall from their pockets down under their feet and past the now stalling bird.

In the kitchen their mother is sitting, belly swelled with a new sister who will be here soon and will be called Norah. She will be more strong-willed than both of her sisters combined and have the finest, blonde hair. She will also love to sing, and amongst the family there will be surprise at how much determination she has. The girls barge into the house. Both in tears.

'What's wrong, girls?'

'Emily got bit by a swan!' says Olivia.

'Where did it bite ya?'

'On the leg,' Emily manages to say.

The mother rubs her daughter's thigh. 'Why did it bite you, did you do something to it?'

Olivia is settling now. 'She threw acorns at it and it chased us, I thought we were dead.'

The mother starts to laugh. 'Emily, did you throw acorns at the swan?'

She nods and cries all the more.

'Well, you wouldn't like people to throw stuff at you, would you?'

Emily shakes her head.

'Right, into the living room the both of you, I'll make you a glass of juice and get you a biscuit and everything will be alright.'

After a few minutes, eyes are dried up from tears. They watch cartoons on the television. Biscuits half-eaten. Orange juice already done. Emily finds an acorn in her pocket, examines it down by her side, then puts it back in her pocket again.

'What time does the park close, Olivia?'

'Dunno, Emily.'

Part Two

Part Two

Sellotape

I feel woozy when I wake. Heavy. Brush my teeth, wash my face. Get ready for school. My morning ritual. In the kitchen, Uncle Bubbles stands by the toaster. Likes to catch the slices as they spring into the air. His morning ritual.

'Mornin'.' He says.

'Mornin'.' I sit at the table. Rest my forehead on my arms. Hear the clunk of jack-in-the-box toast. Scratch-scratch of the buttering knife. I am too tired to care.

A clicking sound follows him across the tile floor. What is that noise?

'Shift yourself.' I glance up. He sets the plate down in front of me. Loiters. 'What's up with ya?'

'I've a light head, Uncle Bubbles.'

He laughs. 'Will take more than a light head to take a day aff school.'

'I'll still go.' I am trying to learn to man up. But don't feel like going.

'You're bloody right ya will!' He heads for the sink. Clicks as he walks. 'Do ya want tay?'

'No thanks.'

'You'll be grand once ya get outside,' he looks into the back garden, 'take a couple or three big breaths of fresh air.'

I chew the toast slowly. Feel awful. Something has brewed in me overnight. The only thing keeping me lucid now is this strange clicking, which I determine to be coming from Uncle Bubbles's right boot. He doesn't mention it, so neither do I. Doesn't take much to set him off. *I know better.*

When I sling on my backpack and head out into the street, a thin fog tiptoes through the hedged gardens and I draw a large breath as instructed. It goes in alright, but comes out uneasily. You know there's something wrong when your breathing is shaky.

By the time the bus journey is over and I have gone into school, two different people have said to me, 'You're as white as a sheet.'

I *feel* pale. Also warm. Make it through the first hour, until I can take no more and raise my hand and ask to see the school nurse. Mr. Johnston, old grumpy bollocks himself, takes two steps toward me. His eyes narrow. 'You *are* pale, Lappin.'

A tilt of his head authorises me to leave and before I

am through the door, he continues teaching the class. The corridor floor is shiny and makes me squint. I knock. She is there. A stout lady with arms like Popeye who could peel through a barrel of spuds without breaking sweat. She places a hand on the side of my neck. 'You are very warm, son.' Her touch, that small human act, reminds me of mother. When the nurse discovers I am running a temperature, she leaves the room to telephone Uncle Bubbles and I expect nothing more than to be kept in school, but she returns with paracetamol and a glass of water. 'Take this and then wait outside. Your uncle is coming to collect you.'

I wait on the wooden bench by the entrance door. It is still cold. Sky blue. Enough for a woollen hat and gloves. Definitely a coat. But I sit with my jacket off and welcome the invisible freeze against my skin. Uncle Bubbles will probably come to pick me up, then bollock me all the way home.

It's hard at thirteen years old to man up. Something that is new to me. But I am trying, ever since the last time I cried and he grabbed my shoulders. Told me to *man up, son! man up!*

I have just started to goose-bump, when Uncle Bubbles pulls up in his rusty blue car and yanks the handbrake. He gets out. Clicks as he walks. Must be a stone. Stuck in the under-grooves of his boot.

The expression he bears is not one I've seen before, not on him anyway. Eyes softened. Brow lifted slightly.

Resembles some kind of concern. He reminds me of mother, just in that moment, and after eight months of living with him, this is the first time.

'Come on, son.' He lifts my backpack as though I am too sick to do so myself. Opens the door. Waits for me to climb in.

On the way home his music blares. The Eagles. He puffs a cigarette and it sneaks into my throat, wraps smoky strings around my lungs, pulls tight. He stops off at the shop. I wind down a window. The sun has come up and the sky is clear.

When we turn into our street, frost holds firm on the green where the small kids play. He stops at the kerb. Removes keys from the ignition. Jingles them in his hand. 'Right. Go lie down on the sofa so I can keep an eye on you.'

I don't want to lie on the sofa. But I do. He comes in with a blanket and drapes it around me. I didn't know Uncle Bubbles could be tender. He leaves the room. Returns with a glass of Lucozade. Nectar for the sick.

'Sip at that. Sleep if ya like.' He scratches the back of his hand. Then a finger. 'I'll be busy here for a while.'

I lie and watch him first hoover the living room carpet, then sit in his lounge chair and smoke a cigarette. If I had the energy I would open a window. He itches at his thumb this time. Rubs it up and down his trouser leg.

'The hands playing up?' I say.

'They are.' He says. 'They're going to break out in that

bloody rash again. I can feel it in ma water.'

I close my eyes for what seems only like moments and awake to the sound of a muffled *scratch-scratch-scratch.* Pause. *Scratch-scratch-scratch.* I imagine a dog pawing at the sofa, wanting to get up and lick me. We never owned a dog. My sister Maria was bitten as a child and remains frightened of them to this day. Well, I assume so. Been four months since I last saw her. I open my eyes. Was I dreaming? Uncle Bubbles is on his hands and knees on the floor with his back to me. Am I still dreaming? I spy a golden drawing pin stuck to the sole of his right boot.

'What're you doing there, Uncle Bubbles?'

He raises onto his knees. Twists toward me. 'Cleaning the carpet.' He holds up a slender metal blade with rows of tiny teeth. 'Hacksaw blade. Takes a while, but this lifts everything.'

'Doesn't the hoover do that?' I notice a neat bundle of fluff on the ground.

'Hoover only takes the rough aff it. Rest yourself there now.'

I lie back down. Doze. *Scratch-scratch-scratch.* Feel terrible. *Scratch-scratch-scratch.* In my hazy swirl of thoughts I wonder if you can beat a sickness by manning up. A strange feeling needles my stomach. I try to ignore it.

When I wake again, he is gone, but I hear him click around the kitchen tiles. He comes in and sits. Lights a cigarette. His leg bounces uncontrollably.

'What ya think of the floor?'

I glance down. It looks no different. 'Looks good.'

'How ya feelin'?'

'Like shite.' It is out before I can think not to say it. First time I've sworn in front of him. I haven't the energy to prepare myself for his onslaught.

'Ya look it too.' He scratches his hand. Winces.

'Did you put your cream on?'

'The cream is a loada crap.' He rubs the back of his hand up and down the arm of the chair. 'Itching like crazy today.'

'I thought about your itchy hands one night in bed, Uncle Bubbles, and wondered, what if we wrapped them up in something. Would that soothe them?'

'Wrap them up ya say? In what?'

'That's the bit I wasn't sure about. All I could think of was sellotape.'

He nods. Sits for a moment, then rises and leaves.

I hear him click into the kitchen, open a drawer. Close it.

He comes back in. 'Here.' Hands me a roll of sellotape.

I sit up. That pain in my stomach again. 'You think it will work?'

'I'll try anythin'.'

He holds out a hand and I begin to wrap the tape around it, pulling it between his fingers. Under. Over.

Creak. Crinkle. Schlape.

'Cover it all now. Right up to the wrist.'

Creak. Crinkle. Schlape. Schlape.

One hand done. He clenches his fist. Opens it. 'Ya know, it doesn't itch. This is great! Do the other one.'

I go at the other hand with the tape too, until he sits there in his armchair like someone who should be locked in an asylum. He closes his eyes. Rests his head back. 'Such relief. Such a great idea.'

I lie down again. Feel like I could sink into the sofa. Beyond that. Sink into the earth itself. Down into the soil. Down and down.

'So I was right? It works?' My voice croaks.

'Doesn't itch one bit. Feels great. Thanks, son. I didn't realise ya were as smart.'

While I am in his good grace, I think to bring up something else. 'You've a drawing pin stuck in the sole of your boot there. I noticed it when you were doing the carpet.

He lifts his foot up. Examines it.

'The other one.'

He checks the other foot. 'Where the hell did that come from?' He raises his taped hands. 'Pull it out or ma.'

I claw in around it. Can't get my nails underneath. I open my backpack and take out a ruler. Slide it under. Pop. I set it on the table.

He stands. Clenches his sellotaped hands. Opens them. Leaves the room.

I don't know how long I sleep on the sofa, but it is fluctuating and unsettled, spinning with pain and unease.

The house is static and full of quiet. No clicking boot. No wrecking about. He must be out in the garden or away for a nap.

'Wake up! Wake up will ya!' His sellotaped hands are on my shoulders. 'Ya wee shit! Get this aff me!'

I sit up. Try to wake.

'They're itchin' like mad! Ma hands are on fire! Take this aff right now!'

I begin to pick at the tape.

'Get the scissors!'

I stumble from the sofa. My body tremoring. Go to the kitchen. Feel like I will faint. Open a drawer. Another. No scissors.

'Would ya hurry up!' He is behind me. 'Ya wee shit! Get this aff!'

'I can't find the scissors!'

'Get a knife then! Move!' He shoves past. I don't have the energy for this. He pulls the drawer so hard the whole thing comes off its rails. Everything spills to the floor.

'The big bread one.' He points frantically with a plasticky finger. 'Grab that.'

I lift the knife. Unsure what to do.

'Hurry up will ya! Slide it under here, at the wrist.'

I tease it in, and begin to saw gently.

'Get it aff!'

The sellotape starts to come away. I pull at it.

'Cut here! Pull it!'

One hand is free. A deep red. He gnaws at the skin

with his teeth. I start into other one. Cutting. Tugging. In around his fingers the tape is well stuck and I yank it hard.

Then a crimson trickle. In the gap between two knuckles.

'Jesus son!' His eyes are wide.

I can't believe I've cut him. What have I done? My head starts to circle in a slow arc, Uncle Bubbles grabs a tea towel. Holds it against his hand. Red seeps through. The floor rushes to meet my face. I feel cold tiles. See shreds of wrinkled tape. Cutlery. Cooking implements.

He kneels beside me. 'Son? Are ya alright, son?'

He is tapping my face. I can barely feel it. 'Do ya need ma to call the doctor?'

Phone in his hand. I see him shaking. His voice falls quieter as though someone is turning down the volume.

Silence.

His blood.

Everything black.

The Cowboy

It was rumoured the farmer who lived in the house with the twelve chimneys had a set of medieval stocks in one of his rundown sheds, and that trespassers caught on his land would be bundled into his tractor and taken to be put in those stocks and dear knows what else.

Boon often stood in *The Bunch of Grapes* listening to such tales and watching them pass from one cigarette curl to another, as faces leaned in around tables then burst into glorious arrays of white teeth and laughter. He liked to loiter at the bar. Watch beer stream like honey into tilted glasses.

'The Ginger Whinger telling his tales again?' Gregory the barman straightened up the pint. Levelled off the foamy head. 'There you go.'

'Aye. I'm getting a minute's head peace here 'til he comes back from the bog.' Boon took a sip. 'Ah sure, here he comes now.'

'As I was saying,' a small man with a freckled face and rich ginger hair climbed onto the stool beside Boon. Lifted a pint of Guinness. Slurped at the foam. 'I mean, everyone knows old Billy the Goat Hawthorne went blind in his sleep, but that's not the full story.'

'Aye, some fellas were talking about it yesterday in here,' said Gregory. 'I wouldn't mind *too much* going blind myself, at least I wouldn't have to look at your ugly mugs, but if I ever lost my hearing…that would be a complete bollocks. Imagine not being able to listen to music.'

'Now that's a dilemma alright,' said Boon.

The Ginger Whinger downed half his Guinness. 'Apparently, Billy the Goat got caught years ago, put into the farmer's stocks. Was locked in them for six days. No food. No water. And the things that got done to him.'

'What's that got to do with him going blind in his sleep?'

'Well, wait until you hear this. He got out of the stocks after six days of God-knows-what. Same night. Goes blind in his sleep. Too much of a coincidence for me that.'

Gregory stood nodding. Arms folded.

Boon sipped his pint. Smiled. 'I haven't heard that one before now.'

'And then there was that Russian fella, what was his name?' Gregory shook a finger.

'Sergei,' said the Ginger Whinger.

'That's it. Sergei. Sure he ended up in the stocks too. Think he was caught stealing turf. After he got out , he moved to New Zealand. Imagine. To the other side of the world!'

'I'd move to New Zealand maself to get away from you clampits.' Boon shook his head. Drank some beer.

'No that's not right, Gregory,' said the whinger, 'I heard Sergei ended up in a lunatic asylum down in Dublin. His whole mind just went. He's sitting down there somewhere right now drooling down himself.'

'If you drink much more of thon black stuff you'll be drooling down yerself.' Boon finished his pint. Headed for the door.

As he strolled home he thought about his plundering of the farmer's crops. It had been two years or so. The stories hadn't put him off. They were just wild imagination and drink talking anyway. Nobody he knew had actually seen the supposed medieval stocks. So he did what any reasonable person would do and brushed them away like a crumb from a trouser leg.

The house was in darkness except for a weak lamp that his granny liked to leave on for him in the kitchen and Boon paused on the back doorstep, his favourite spot to smoke a final cigarette before bed. The moon sat low over roofs of distant houses and as he observed its pale sickle he wondered when old Billy the Goat Hawthorne had last seen a moon.

He opened the door. Removed his boots and left them

where they fell. He yawned and felt hungry then, but couldn't be bothered to make something, so pulled a little trick from his back pocket that he used once in a while. Boon turned off the lamp. Toppled a chair as loudly as he could. Waited for any sound upstairs. When nothing came, he did the same again, this time crying out as though in terrible pain. He heard the creak of the bed. Footsteps. The click of the light-switch.

By the time she came down, Boon had arranged himself on the floor with the sideways chair on top of his body. The kitchen door opened. Light came on.

'My God, son! Are you alright?' She was in her robe. Hair netted. Curlers.

'Ahh granny, I've wrecked maself! You must've forgotten to leave the light on again.' He held an arm out for some help.

As she gripped and helped him to his feet, Boon did some pretend wincing.

'I was sure I had left it on for you, son.'

'Sure never worry about it. Can't remember everything at your age. You go on back to bed and I'll clean this up.' Boon lifted the chair. Set it back upon its feet. Dusted himself off even though there was nothing to dust. 'I'm gonna make a cup of tea to settle my nerves, do you want one?'

'I'll make it, son.'

'Sure why don't you throw on some toast too while you're at it? And maybe some bacon.'

'Alright son.'

As he waited for the bacon, his mind drifted back to the beginning. The apple orchard.

Boon had kept an eye on the local paper for the farmer's advertisement to appear calling for summer pickers. That black rectangle filled with words said one thing to most people, but to him it whispered crooked code that the apples were ripe and ready to be stolen before pickers showed up and snipped through the orchard like an army of crabs.

In those early days, Boon would have taken just enough apples for himself and his grandmother who appreciated the ingredients for making her tarts, until he stopped off in the pub one night and set a bag of apples at his feet.

'What've you got there?' The Ginger Whinger leaned forward on his stool.

'A policeman wouldn't even ask me that. Apples.'

'You selling them?'

'Nope. Why are you after some?'

'I'd buy a bag of apples at the right price. Where'd you get them from?'

'None of yer business. A friend of mine.'

'Don't suppose your friend could get his hands on a few sacks of logs?'

Soon, he had a shopping list. First for half the pub. A few months later, half the village. Everyone knew Boon was good on this word, especially those who bought the cheap cigarettes he got from Johnny O'Lachlin.

As the air around him grew thick with momentum, Boon's attention soon wandered to other parts of the farmer's lands. He had come across a lake that was good for illegal fishing all year round and not long after that, discovered two small fields where the farmer grew neat rows of strawberries. He knew about the farmer's poultry pen and although not adverse to plundering it, kept it purely for financial or hunger-related emergencies. Boon had even been so bold as to take a few milk churns from the big yard up by the house where the farmer parked his tractors.

His granny set down a plate of toast and bacon. A mug of tea. 'I'm going back to bed, son.'

'Alright, granny. Thanks.' Boon took a bite. Pictured the wooden stocks in his mind and then laughed.

In his complex calendar, which only existed inside his head, Boon knew the ins and outs of the farmer's crops, which fields would be in use at any given time, and which produce would prosper next. He also had a mental list of clientele along with details of what they'd be interested in buying. Most of the auld dolls in the village, for instance, would be keen on Boon's apples. Oblivious to where he got them from. Most men were interested in the sacks of logs he sold from a trailer around September time. For cheap fuel bills. To keep their wives cosy and happy.

In order to fill up the trailer, Boon would usually spend a few hours angling in the farmer's lake, then wrap whatever sad-mouthed fish he had caught in newspaper, to take home for his grandmother. On his way back through the fields, he'd take a detour through the forest to check for logs stacked on top of one another like giant cigars. As soon as they appeared, Boon rubbed his hands. Started to calculate the orders. Then returned every day to see whether the farmer had chopped them into woody coins because that saved him the hassle of doing it himself. Boon would accumulate enough wood to fuel his grandmother's fire right through the winter, with plenty left over for bagging and selling to anyone who would buy a cheap sack of logs.

Boon finished his bacon sandwich. Emptied his pockets onto the kitchen table. A roll of banknotes. Elastic band around them. A penknife. A guitar pick. He began unravelling the money. Then counting it.

Aside from the farmer's land, Boon's main source of income was creeping lorry loads of illegal tobacco over the border for Johnny O'Lachlin. The money was good at a hundred quid per run. And he could buy cigarettes cheaper than anyone else then sell them on. Even though Boon didn't like working for someone else and certainly didn't like to be micro-managed, a man still had to make a living and tobacco runs were easy money. Aside from the risk.

In his grandmother's house, Boon found shortcuts around things too. He had discovered that if done discreetly enough, he could run an electrical wire from the mains under the stairs, hide it under the soil in the garden, and permanently connect it into the streetlight outside. Render his electric bill a practical zero. Sometimes he sat in front of the television, drinking his grandmother's tea and just chuckling to himself about all of the free electricity he could waste at his leisure.

◈   ◈   ◈

One evening in *The Bunch of Grapes*, Boon came in and sat on a barstool and listened to a heavily bearded gentleman's conversation with Gregory.

'They're a goldmine these houses. Ma mate gets the call soon after the old person kicks the bucket, then in he goes, clears everything out. All the while, pilfering furniture, antiques. Selling them on.'

'Excuse me fella, you wouldn't have a cigarette would you?' Boon liked to size people up this way. It told him what he needed to know about their depth of character.

'Surely. Here you go.'

'Thanks.' Boon lit it up. Took a draw. 'You know, don't think I like this idea of pillaging old people while their breath still hangs in the air. What would you call it... their *death mist*. Every man should have at least some principles.'

The bearded fellow nodded. Lifted a cheek. Broke wind.

'Speaking of wind,' said Boon. 'Did you hear it last night, fella?'

'Hear it? Was so stormy the slates on the roof played like a piano.' He swigged from his pint. 'Aye, ma mate is into everything. Fake bank notes, Grave-robbing.'

Though violating cemeteries was something Boon had never tried, he considered the money that could be made from a bag of gold teeth and it was a thought he would hold onto for another day. He held out his hand. 'Don't think we've met. I'm Boon.'

'They call me Sweaty.' He shook Boon's hand. 'Ma mate was telling me about the farmer around here. The one with the stocks. Surely that's not true?'

'Oh it's true alright,' said Gregory. 'Apparently he's real straight-laced too. Doesn't drink or anything.'

'Sure how could you trust a man that doesn't drink?'

Gregory leaned on the counter. 'They say he doesn't leave his own land, except to go to church. And even then, there's a tunnel from his big house, under the cemetery. Right into the church itself.'

'That's some fairytale,' said Sweaty.

Boon nodded. 'I've heard that one too.'

'Well, ma mate's told me all sorts of stories about people getting put in these stocks, so I'll be staying clear of thon farmer. To think I nearly got caught maself one time stealing his rhubarb. Didn't even realise whose land I was on!'

'Rhubarb you say? I didn't know he grew rhubarb.' Boon stubbed out his cigarette. He thought he knew every inch of those lands, yet here was rhubarb he had never stolen. And his grandmother loved rhubarb.

'Oh aye. Does surely. Massive big field of it.'

'Where would that be now?'

The directions he got were hazy because Sweaty was drunk and they almost didn't make any sense at all, but if there was farmer's produce to be had, Boon would soon find it.

That following morning, Boon sat at the kitchen table he had inherited from someone he wasn't related to, wearing two odd socks and drinking tea made by his grandmother that was brewed twice and strong as liquor. He instructed her to throw on some toast and she rustled around the kitchen in her flower-print apron, before landing three slices of marmaladen toast in front of him. As she rubbed around the countertops with a cloth, stopping every so often to swipe crumbs into her hand, Boon asked if she had gotten the chance to clean his wellington boots.

'I have, son. Hold on.' She dropped crumbs into the swing bin. Fumbled in a cupboard under the stairs. Set the boots right at his feet.

'Thanks Granny.'

'You're welcome son. Will you be back for dinner?'

'Aye. Hope you're making me something nice?'

She chuckled, a little embarrassed. 'I'll put something together.'

'I might be going out later on, Granny. Can you find me some jeans and clean socks?'

'Yes son.'

'Thanks. You know what, you're going to get a great birthday present next month,' Boon pointed both fingers at her, 'because you deserve it.'

'If God spares me.' Her yellow marigolds squeaked as she wiped the same countertops over again.

'Oh he'll spare you alright, no doubt about that. You have to reach the big eight-o.'

'Well, with his grace. We'll see.'

Boon pulled on his green wellington boots and the black cowboy hat someone had left behind in the pub one night. As he set off, his grandmother followed him outside. Began to scratch the giant yard brush across the grey concrete.

He followed a lane that was sometimes good for blackberries if the children hadn't got to them first, then after fifty yards or so, climbed over the fence at his favourite spot. As always, he took a few moments to survey the horizon for any sign of the farmer. Adjusted the cowboy hat and set off. He had started wearing it on the farmer's land as a decoy, knowing if the farmer ever had reports of a trespasser, the description of a man wearing a cowboy hat would not only sound ridiculous, but could also never be traced back to him because he never wore it anywhere else. They'd never catch him.

This first field was good for potatoes two years out of every three and Boon made a small fortune selling them in sacks. When the farmer let the field rest or grew corn instead, it put a dent in Boon's income and he'd wait patiently for the spuds to be planted again.

After crossing another couple of fields, Boon neared the forest and thought he heard the chug of a tractor. He crouched down. Waited. Lifted a smooth stone out of the muck. When all seemed quiet again, he dropped the stone and moved into the forest. Headed for the lake. A ten minute walk.

In among the trees it was dark and quiet, and as he climbed over a fallen tree, Boon recalled the time he had arrived at the lake with his fishing rod and there, tied to a newly spouted post, was a white-painted rowboat with a single flat seat across its middle. He had considered stealing and selling it on back then, but it went against his business strategy. Taking one dry stalk from a haystack was not noticeable, but thieving the whole haystack was. He had also thought briefly about using it for fishing, but thought how difficult escape might be if the farmer ever showed up. So he had fished from the grass as normal and tried his best to ignore the boat and its potential sale price.

Boon came out of the forest and into the light, to find that today the lake was calm enough. The odd wind grating its surface. He had been here three days ago. Caught a pike the length of his arm. He loved spoiling his grandmother with fresh pike, though most people regarded them not meant for eating.

Passing the lake, he cut through the orchard and found

the drunken directions given by Sweaty had fizzled out. He stood still for a while, scanning hedges, looking for the mysterious lane that had been described to him, then took off the cowboy hat. Scratched the top of his head. Put it back on again. It was only by walking right past it, that he found a badly overgrown lane he had never noticed before. Boon moved carefully through brambles and nettles as high as his shoulders. Eventually found himself standing in a square field full of rhubarb. Sweetness filling the air. Giant green leaves spreading out like lily pads on a lake. He bent down to crack a stalk, then sniffed and examined it, before producing a folded-up sack from his pocket. As he hunkered down and began to yank, then stuff the red stalks into his sack, he could hear the sound of his own breath and suddenly realised how quiet this particular field was. Boon stood up and listened for a moment.

Not a sound. No wind, no birds, no nothing.

He removed the cowboy hat and wiped his brow, then thought he heard something. He knelt down. A trickle of sweat found its way out from his hairline and down into his right eyebrow. He dried his face with the inside of an elbow. Dropped the hat in amongst the rhubarb. His heart beat faster than normal and he waited a full two minutes before realising it was nothing.

Getting back to the picking, Boon soon had his sack full to the brim. He heard a strange click. Turned around.

'Hold it right there,' said the farmer. 'This is a pepper

gun. It won't kill ya, but it'll hurt like hell.'

Boon took off, hopping quickly through the rhubarb. Birds suddenly splashed across the sky and he took a face full of giant leaves. The pain gnarled his buttocks. Like sitting in a chair that was on fire. Then he rolled a little, squashing and breaking stalks, until the clunk of a gun butt smashed into his shoulder.

◈   ◈   ◈

A strong smell filled his nostrils. As his eyes opened, it felt like a guillotine had dropped directly onto his rear-end.

He was looking down. Into a bucket of cow dung, brown and watery.

All at once, Boon felt the clamp around his head. Locks around each wrist. Panic set in. His whole body shook. The medieval stocks stayed as still as iron. He tried to stand up even, to lift the entire contraption off the ground, but it would not budge and his ass ached.

Glancing up, as much as the stocks would allow his neck to strain, Boon saw that he was in a large shed and just as he began to swear, the heavy doors scraped open. Boon looked up to see the farmer's wellington boots. Black. Scuffed with muck.

'So…ya think it's alright ta steal another man's livelihood, do ya?'

'Aye, and you think it's alright to shoot people!'

'Oh ya can shoot a thief no bother, law allows it.'

'Well, you may add bloody kidnapping as well, cause that's what this is!'

The farmer pulled out a three-legged stool. Sat facing Boon. 'Ya know, the last fella I had in these, was in them fer a week. That's how long it took'em ta say sorry. Ya wouldn't want ta know what happened ta'em. I'll let ya find that out fer yerself.'

'Sorry? Look I'm sorry, no bother. Sure what's a bit of rhubarb?' To fill the silence Boon continued to speak. 'I'll pay you for it no problem, just tell me much it costs and I'll square you up.'

'Are you the one they call the cowboy?' asked the farmer, squinting.

Boon thought quickly, the cowboy hat, where was the cowboy hat...

'No way. I'm just an honest man trying to gather a bit of rhubarb for my granny. She loves baking the tarts. I tell you what, I'll get her to bake you one, how about that?'

'Because I think about that cowboy when I'm lyin' in bed at night. Think about puttin' his balls in a vice. Turnin' the handle. I hear things ya know. I'm not stupid. They talk about'em down at the meat market. He touches no-one else's land. Only mine. Rumour has it he's been plunderin' my crops for a long, long time and I've a bone ta pick with'em. Thing is, I think yer the cowboy.'

Boon remembered he took the hat off. It was still in

the rhubarb field. 'I'm no cowboy!' His mind darted. Words spilled out. 'I've heard of the fella you're talking about though. He comes into the pub now and again, so I believe. And he steals from your land, is that right now?'

'Oh he does indeed.' The farmer pulled out a brown, tatty notebook from his trouser pocket that had a black outline of a cow on its cover. 'See I've been makin' a list over the past year or so of the things I'm gonna do ta this cowboy once I catch'em and put'em in the stocks. So if yer him, I'd ba just about ta start inta number two in the list.'

'Number two? Sure what's number one, shoot an innocent fella!'

'Number one is the bucket of cow dung that yer lookin' into right now. Yer going ta be takin' a good long drink from it. Number two, is…' The farmer consulted his notebook. 'Heatin' up the cattle brand til it's roarin' red hot, then stampin' my mark onta ya. Cause ya belong ta me now.'

'Well you needn't bother with your list, for I'm not him. How many times have I gotta tell you? Maybe you know my granny? That might vouch for something? Edna Rusket.'

The farmer got up. Paced about. Tugged at his lower lip. 'Edna Rusket's yer granny?'

'Aye, she is. Great woman. Look, my neck's nearly broke here. Get me out of this bloody thing!' Boon waited for a response. Watched the farmer's wellies walk up and down.

'How's she keepin'?'

'She's doing the very best, turns eighty in a couple weeks' time. Honestly, I was just talking to some fella in the pub and asking where I could get some rhubarb for my granny and he gave me directions to your rhubarb field.'

'And was this fella ya were talking ta, the same one ya say is the cowboy?'

'I've an *idea* who the cowboy is. But look, if you want to catch him, you'd be better getting down to the pub, that's where he probably hangs out. You know, suss him out.'

'I don't go inta pubs. They're fulla the devil's buttermilk! Nothin' but gateways ta hell itself!'

Boon dropped his head for a few seconds. Looked up again. 'You know what you need? A ranger.'

'What sorta ranger?'

'A ranger to walk your lands, keep an eye on things, look out for the cowboy. I could do it. All I'd need was that pepper gun you like to shoot people with and a wage.'

'I'd love ta catch that cowboy so I could get'em inta the stocks and start inta ma list. It's three pages long so far...'

The farmer flipped pages back and forth briefly. 'Look at this. Number thirteen. Ma favourite. One by one, smash his fingertips with a hammer.' He closed the notebook and tapped it off his fingers, then walked over and lifted away the bucket of manure.

'Now listen! Don't you be starting into that list! I'm no cowboy, you hear!' Boon heard the click of latches. His eyeballs became wide and bulging.

'I'm lettin' ya go because of yer grandmother. She worked at the house here when I was a boy. Ya tell her I was askin' about her.'

'Is that right? No problem, I'll tell her.'

'Oh and one more thing,' said the farmer.

'What's that now?'

'If ya get ma that cowboy. I'll give ya five grand.'

Boon tried to stand and fell down. 'I'd do it for six.' He managed to get up and held out his hand. The farmer shook it.

'Ya'll do it for five and ba thankful yer still breathin'.'

'Don't worry. I'll get him for you. I'm a man of my word.'

Boon hobbled his way back to the rhubarb field, feeling strange to be an authorised person who no longer had to worry about getting caught or seen or shot by the farmer. After gathering his rhubarb and stuffing in a few more stalks, he lifted the cowboy hat, hid it under his jacket and headed on home.

◈　　　　　　◈　　　　　　◈

The first week on the job was easy. Boon spent most of

it roaming the farmer's lands to acquaint himself with parts he'd never seen before, trying to establish if there was something he hadn't stolen, but could now make money from. He was happy not to have to look over his shoulder.

To please the farmer, Boon said he had seen the cowboy from a distance, but when he shouted, the cowboy ran off. The farmer had fire in his eyes. Boon also made up a story about some kids trying to steal apples and that impressed the farmer too.

As time went on though, the farmer started to get annoyed that there were no more sightings of the cowboy, and when Boon made some up, the farmer would get excited momentarily, then frustrated that the cowboy still hadn't been apprehended.

After a few weeks, Boon began to come under pressure for results. The cowboy needed to be caught.

On the way home one Friday evening, Boon stopped off at the pub for a pint. As he debated going home to his dinner or ordering another pint, in walked Sweaty looking all gloomy.

'Greg. Give'us a triple bush. In fact, just fill the whole glass.'

'Dear dear. What's ruffled your feathers?'

'Lost ma bloody job is what.'

'Ah sure, you'll always get another one.'

'Easier said than done.' He gulped at the whiskey. Hung his head. Stared into the bar.

As Boon watched the pain in his face, it suddenly reminded him of being shot in his rear-end. And as Sweaty was the one who had directed him to the rhubarb field in the first place, Boon would hold him indirectly responsible.

'Say, how would you like to earn an easy forty quid?'

'How's that now?'

'All you have to do is wear a cowboy hat and let me pretend I've caught you on the farmer's land. Once he takes you back to the big shed, he'll put you in the stocks and –'

'Hold on here, these stocks are real?'

'Oh they're real alright and I've been in them. No big deal. As soon as you say sorry, he lets you out, but you have to mean it.'

'I'll have to think about it, I could use the money…'

'Look I'll give you *fifty* quid and two sacks of spuds. You're out of work now, why turn down opportunities to earn? It'll take you an hour at most. Who makes fifty quid an hour that doesn't work in London? You tell me? All you have to do is meet me on Monday afternoon. Around two. Let's say out by the farmer's lake. We'll get the cowboy hat on you. Take you to the farmer to say sorry.'

Sweaty finished his drink. Looked at Boon. 'Fifty quid?'

'Yep.'

'Alright. Forget the spuds.' Sweaty stood up. 'If there's

another glass of bush waiting when I get back from the bog, we've got a deal.' He patted Boon's shoulder as he passed.

'Gregory. Get that man another bush.' Boon smiled. 'Why do they call him Sweaty anyway?'

'Comes from his surname,' said Gregory.

'And what's that now?'

'Balls.'

◈   ◈   ◈

Boon woke up on Saturday morning feeling like he had caught a cold, so lay around the house all weekend giving orders to his grandmother. After a spell in bed, a stain on the ceiling irritated him so much, that his grandmother offered to paint over it. So she got up on the stepladder and painted over it, but the new paint didn't blend right with the old paint, so he had her redo the whole ceiling. Afterwards, Boon's irritation was gone and he felt so pleased, that he allowed her to run herself a bath and relax for the evening.

On Monday, the sun came out. Sky sea-blue in among the clouds. Boon still felt poorly, but the cowboy had to be caught, so off he went across the fields towards the farmer's lake.

When he arrived, Sweaty was in the farmer's boat, rowing himself around.

'What the hell are you doing?' shouted Boon, in his

loudest whisper.

Sweaty laughed, rowing then with one oar, like a bird with an injured wing. Making chirping noises. He clambered out of the boat. Splashed Boon's jeans.

'Will you watch what you're at!' Boon handed him the cowboy hat, 'Here put this on.'

Sweaty put on the hat and began to sing, 'Ya picked a fiyne tiyme to leeve me...Loo-seal...'

Boon laughed. 'You're about to be put in the famous stocks and you're mucking about! I wish I was as confident as you.'

He stood behind the fake cowboy and pointed the pepper gun at his back. 'Right, just walk and it'll look like I've caught you. When we get to the yard, try to look a bit scared and remember the main thing is once you're in the stocks, to say sorry and mean it. Okay?'

'Let's go,' said Sweaty. 'This is the easiest fifty quid I've ever earned.'

Boon marched him through the trees for a while until they reached a lane with grass growing up the middle of it like a green mohawk. They walked that for a few minutes before turning left and entering the farmer's yard.

'Look at how many buildings this guy has, he must be loaded!'

'Shush you! Keep walking.'

They passed the big green tractor and went right up to the back door of the farmer's house. Boon tapped the gun tip against the wood three times. Waited for an answer. Just as he considered going on in, he heard something and turned to see the farmer emerge from a shed, carrying a bucket.

When the farmer saw Boon and the cowboy, he stopped right on the spot. Stared. Set down his bucket and came over.

'So ya got'em?'

'Aye, cheeky bollocks was in your rowboat. Couldn't get away.'

The two spoke about the cowboy as if he wasn't there.

'Right, take'em inta the big shed and put'em in the stocks. I'll get ma notebook, it's in the house. I thought of another few ta add ta the list last night.'

'I'm not going in no stocks! Yis can piss off!'

'You'll do as you're told or I'll stick a few bullet holes into you!' said Boon in his best angry voice. Boon marched him off down to the big shed and whispered, 'Good acting big fella.'

Checking the farmer was gone, Boon slid open the huge barn door and they went inside. Sweaty began to laugh. 'I don't believe it! Bloody stocks! Where the hell did he get these from?'

'I don't know, right let's get you into them.' Boon opened one end. Lifted it like a drawbridge. Still laughing, Sweaty put his neck into the half-moon cut and did the same with his hands. Just as Boon closed down the lid and wrestled with the locking mechanism, in walked the farmer. 'I can't seem to lock this, there must be a knack to it.'

The farmer, without speaking, came over and locked the stocks, then gave them a shake to ensure they were secure. He moved around to the front.

'So...the cowboy.' As the farmer interlocked both hands behind his back, he stood up tall. Stared down at his prisoner. 'I've been waitin' a long, long time for this moment...'

Boon tried not to laugh.

'Yev been robbin' ma land fer years!'

Sweaty looked like he might laugh too, then said in his best unenthused voice, 'Look I'm sorry. I won't do it again.' He looked up. Caught Boon's eyes. Wide and scolding.

The farmer pulled out his notebook and turned to Boon. 'Boon, ya did good son. You head on home.'

'Thanks very much, but are you not finished with him, I could escort him off your land?'

'Oh, I won't ba finished with'em for a while yet...I've a long list ta get through here, remember?' The farmer wrapped his notebook off one hand.

'What's this list?' said Sweaty.

'Sure he's said sorry; I don't think he'll be back near your land again.'

'I'm sorry Mr. Farmer, I promise I'll never come on your land again.'

Acting like he hadn't heard anything that had just been

said, the farmer stepped close to Boon. Gave his arm a gentle, funeral squeeze. 'Head on home son, thanks fer the hard work. I'll see ya in the mornin' ta square ya up.'

Boon glanced at the cowboy, then turned and left, sliding the barn door closed behind him.

◈   ◈   ◈

On his way back through the fields, the sky greyed to a corpse. Boon whistled a little before losing enthusiasm for a tune. When he reached home, light rain started to spit the windows and he knew his granny would be out afterwards, wiping them clean. Smeary windows were a sight not to be seen, she always said.

Boon took off his wellingtons at the back door. Went inside. In the living room his grandmother sat knitting. Smiled as he walked in.

'There's a few letters there son, came in the post. Your dinner's in the oven.'

Boon nodded. Began opening letters with a sliding thumb. Most of them were trash. The last one an electric bill. As he stared at the figures, a wry smile snuck onto his face. Disappeared again. It warmed his heart to see a page declaring his bill as zero.

'Electric Bill's in Granny.'

She looked up from her knitting. 'How much do I owe you son? Reach me over my handbag.'

As he handed the old lady her bag, Boon put on his

best *times-are-hard face*. 'It's gone up again Granny, you owe me forty-five quid this time.'

The old woman rustled in her purse. Eventually handed over two twenty pound notes. 'I'll have to owe you a fiver son when I get my pension, is that alright?'

'Aye that's no problem Granny, thanks.' Boon stuffed the notes into his back pocket and the old lady went back to her knitting.

He paused by the door. 'I've had a rough day Granny, can you run me a bath shortly?'

She set aside the knitting and made to get up. 'Sure I'll do it now son, it'll be ready for you finishing your dinner.'

'Alright, thanks. Say, when is your birthday again, tomorrow is it?'

She met him in the doorway, 'It was yesterday, son. When you get to my age birthdays don't matter anymore.'

'I suppose they don't.' He nodded.

The old lady followed her grandson out into the hallway and began to pull all eighty of her years up the wooden hill. Out in the kitchen, Boon opened the oven. Transported a foil-covered plate onto the table. Sat down and unwrapped it. He shook salt and glugged brown sauce over his spuds and as the first mouthful went in, he spotted a freshly baked rhubarb tart on the bench. For a brief moment he thought about the farmer's list. As the second mouthful went in, he had already planned to eat a slice of tart in the bath and get granny to whip up some fresh cream to go with it.

Window

A cloud passes by faster than it should. It is gold trimmed, an expensive one. Now it is gone and my world is still again.

Wait.

The clothesline is dancing. A tiny, imaginary tightrope walker is stepping amongst the pegs. Juggling fiery matchsticks. No, knives. He juggles knives. I can't tell if it's a gentle or blustery wind.

The glass was cleaned yesterday. The man ignored me. Not even a smile, a look in my eye. Already it has that peppery dirt again. How filthy the air must be. Could be the reason I'm here in the first place, but they don't know. All that training and they still don't know.

I've been here so long I notice everything. *Obscure things*. Like that void in the double glaze.

What is in there?

Air?

The trapped breath of whoever made the window?

Now the clothesline is bobbing. Tightrope walker has slipped, hanging on for his life I'd say. Swinging one leg, trying to climb back on.

I haven't seen anyone use that clothesline. Ever.

Now I can't breathe again. I hate this.

◈   ◈   ◈

It's been snowing! I can feel it in my feet. Four days I was under. So they tell me. That's the longest yet.

It's gone dark outside and my window is diminished. Steamed up mostly. If I strain enough, I can see the sill. Looks like marshmallow. I'd love some marshmallow. I wonder if the tightrope walker made it, if he's still there, hanging on, frozen into a little icicle? Or fallen? Shattered into a thousand pieces?

I need him to reach my sill. Climb in the window. He would be useful for me. One of his juggling knives could chip my pencil into a fine point.

Would save my energy.

Someone's been chewing the end. Who would have done such a thing?

Were they sitting there, watching me?

Watching and chewing?

◈   ◈   ◈

I feel weak today. It's bright out. Still snowy. The sky is heavy like a blanket of chains. When I go, I'd like there to be snow on the ground. I want the tiny tightrope man to shimmy up these tubes onto my face and pull shut my eyelids. Then they'll know I'm gone for good.

Ultreia

You place a hand inside each boot and are thankful they are dry. You lace them up and take a moment to stretch both calves, before slinging on your red rucksack and stepping out into the fresh morning with its faded stars and pink sky. You pause to take in the beginnings of a new day, and still, the sun has not yet risen, nor the moon left the sky.

Before long you find the path flowing underfoot like a dry riverbed and you think about all of those who have walked this ancient way. You know by now that it is more than a path, because it can change from hour to hour, and from day to day.

You tread and breathe, one foot then the other. Notice the awakening sky, its slow yawn into pastel blue, its broad halo of orange and yellow. Out in front, the long shadow of your body stretches along the stony track and you look two storeys tall. Your breath becomes a comforting rhythm and it surprises you how much contentment can be found just from breathing.

The barley fields that run either side of the path, interchange from unripened greens, to golden lakes, to pale fields of almost white. By the time the sun is strong against the back of your neck, your shadow has shortened and the path edges become lined with yellow flowers, twisting their way out through the corn like firecrackers.

You sometimes hear birds in the trees, flutter of wings and rhythmic calls, and if you are lucky, catch a glimpse of them in their temporary perches. The path widens as you pass through a handful of houses with grapevines creeping their porches. A faded sign hangs against a plain stone wall. You enter into a bar to rest a little. Enjoy some coffee, a soft fresh croissant.

When you leave, the sky is rich beyond comprehension. Deep and cobalt. Simple yet luxurious. Cornfields give way to tall grass, complemented now and then with white daisies whose petals have waned overnight and only just begun to look for the sun.

You see a figure in the distance, sitting by the side of the path and as you pass you see the lethargy in his face. Sweat in his white hair. He nods. Smiles. 'Warm vandaag.'

You wonder what language it is. Reach into your rucksack and give him a paraguayo. Smile. Pat his shoulder. He laughs a little and takes a bite. You wonder what a man this age is doing here. How his bones are still holding together.

He waves you off. Has a contemplative spirit about him, so you name him *the painter*.

Walking has become the melody of your life. You approach hills that are long and steady. Rise up through their dry beaten paths to find large cream cows standing in their pastures, watching you in unison, with metal bells tinkling their necks. You pass down into a forested valley where a warm wind moves gently through the foliage and the symphonic sound of bells comes back again from animals you can no longer see. You laugh and christen it the musical forest.

'Belle journée pèlerin.' A man turns his head as you approach. Treads slowly with a staff. You walk with him a little. Catch the odd word. Take out your water bottle. Offer it. He has his own but sips yours. Receives your gift.

'Aimerais-tu avoir du chocolat?'

You take a square of his crumpled chocolate bar. Watch the movement of his moustache as he chews a piece. You quietly name him *the chocolatier*. Leave each other with a smile. A handshake. A 'Buen Camino.'

You see now that the people are the path and their souls are linked to yours.

The sun is stronger now. Guiding. Helping you on. Tall poppies multiply as you walk, until you are bordered with a wonderful crimson richness, spreading out into a red sea of beauty all around. You smell the faint perfume and all at once, the flowers are in you, part of you, and you are part of them.

You pause on the track, in the hot afternoon, to catch a breath, to take a drink. It is time to sit, so you take off your rucksack for a few minutes. Eat some bread. Chorizo. You think about the man with the paraguayo, the painter. How tired he was. Whether he found enough strength to keep going, Whether he has already stopped for the day.

The chocolatier was slow, but merry. You imagine him plodding on, through dusk and into darkness. He will keep going until he gets to his destination.

You take a drink of water. Silence settles your being.

When you set off again, the rucksack feels heavier. You know you are waning, the day wearing itself out. Perspiration trickles your brow. As you wipe it away, you are glad for the shade of a tree-lined path and then, although hiding from the world, a small and simple stone church. You stop in the doorway. Place both hands against the cold stone. There is no-one around except the worn statue of a knight either side of the entrance. After cooling a little, you leave.

The path ahead winds through fields like a slung rope and your legs ache at the thought of more walking through these vast and endless lakes. Out in the barley, you catch the flicker of a giant stork lifting off, the majesty of its spread wings pushing against the blue. It crosses the sun. Forces you to squint and look down.

The afternoon fades. Aches settle into your bones. You see a huddle of roofs in the distance and know this is where you will stop for the night. You know that even though the day has been long and filled with your own dusty footsteps, the night will bring food. Then rest. Then resurrection.

She Will Be My Joy

I take an orange from the bowl on the table and head outside. She will be home soon, pushing over the tall hill with cherry in her cheeks and freshness upon her skin, through her hair. I sit on the low wall, in a space that gets the sun, and start into the peel with my thumb. She is the only person I've ever seen that can remove the entire rind in one spiralling piece. Mine is a shred-job, pith and juice all over the place before I can even release the first segment.

A tender breeze sways around me with its scent of cut grass and berries. The farmer has been at work on the pasture and hedgerows all morning, completing his spring trim, leaving pyramidal rows of grass behind the tractor. The iron gate needs some paint. But I know by the time I put on old clothes, find some brushes and a tin of paint, bring them outside and kneel down to begin, it won't be as simple as that, because it never is. The old flakes will probably need to be scraped away. Metal stripped down to a workable surface. There will be something wrong with a hinge. I'll go back through the house and out to the leaning shed to look for a wire brush or a screwdriver and when I make it back to the gate, I will be exhausted and in pain and have to go indoors to lie down.

My life these days has become a series of calculations. Estimating how many steps it might take just to walk across to the field. Stop by its gate. Stroke the old horse. Or trying to work out how I can clean all the windows of the house, how many days it will take and how much energy it will use up.

I eat a piece of orange. She will have left the city by now. High-rises shrinking slowly into old stone buildings. Then there will be nothing but thatch roofs, concrete yards and patchwork fields. Not long until she is here beside me. Sitting. Talking. Being.

The sun reaches down to touch my skin, but still, I am cold all of the time. It is like winter has crawled inside me and decided to rest out the other three seasons until its time has once again come around to prosper. On days when it rains, I sit by the window wishing it would stop, hoping she will get home without a soaking. Sometimes I feel brave and take the black umbrella to meet her off the bus, but by the time I get down the hill and out to the end of the road, I have no energy to get all the way back up again. Though it's worth it, that pain. To see her a little earlier, to lessen her rain.

Today I wait for her here on the wall. Apple and cherry blossoms have begun to sprout in their familiar whites and pinks. Wild daffodils poke out from hedgerows across the way and lean towards the sun to enrich their stems, brighten their yellow. I gather the leathery pieces of rind into a loose pile and close my eyes to rest. My head feels like a till churning through soil. Breath falls shallow. Pain starts to pound up the back of my neck. These moments feel like they can only end in sharp blackness.

◈   ◈   ◈

And she will come. Pushing over the crest and a little out of breath, with a tiny ball of crimson in each of her cheeks. She will catch me sitting there and her head will fall to the side to tell me she is tired. But she will still smile. As she walks, the sun will drench her body in its golden beams and she will stop by the wall and embrace me. Kiss my forehead. I will hear her voice. Smell her hair. Feel the touch of her skin and all of her that comes with it and she will be my joy.

Part Three

The Fight

He was by the sink rubbing his hands with a flowery tea towel when his wife came through the back door wearing a face full of upset. 'Those degenerates have gone too far this time!'

'Not again,' he said, but she was already past him. Heading for the stairs. He moved into the living room where his hand reached into the walnut cabinet that had been in his family for three generations, and came out clutching a bottle of Black Bush. He poured an inch. Took his glass to the sink. Doubled it up with water. He heard her banging above him then. At her records. The familiar silky voice of Ruby Murray began to drift through the ceiling. Always Ruby Murray. He sipped from the crystal rim and ran a hand through his ivory hair. Knew she was up there crying behind the music. His face burned red as he drained the tumbler and set it down into the metal sink.

Before he knew for sure what he would say, he was in the pub and standing in front of McDonagh's table. Shaking a finger. 'No more. Right? Just no more. We're sick of this.'

'Says who?'

'Says me.'

'Who died and elected you mayor?' McDonagh laughed. His table followed.

'I mean it.' He leaned on the table.

'Who's going to stop me exactly? You?' McDonagh laughed again.

He gulped. 'If I have to.'

'Well then.' McDonagh stood up with his dead eyes and leaned on the table himself. 'Why don't we settle this with a fight on Calpenny's bridge, man on man? How about Friday, at half past seven?'

'Right.'

'Right? Is that yes?' McDonagh offered his thick hand.

He shook it and tried to make it home before he might vomit. She was in the living room when he came in. Reading the newspaper. His eye sockets had already blackened to coal and the skin on his face sagged into a colourless shroud.

'I've sorted out McDonagh. Me and him will settle this once and for all.' He nodded, trying to convince himself. She sat and listened. 'I'm fighting him on Friday night at seven thirty. Man on man.'

She took a sharp breath. Page tremored as it turned.

He poured himself a whiskey and tried to relax into the armchair. Thoughts bombarded his brain. He had never had a fight in his life. A dread rose inside him and he drank to quash it.

As her foot tapped the floor like a castanet, he thought hard. Surely there must have been some scuffling in his youth? But he couldn't think of any.

On the Wednesday, he was afraid to leave the house, and by Thursday morning he was a dog that refused to leave its bed. He shuffled from room to room, unable to settle himself and around midday she made vegetable broth that seemed to restore some of the life back into him. He opened up then, as he tore apart some bread and dipped it through the steam.

'I mean, I can't really believe I agreed to such a thing.' She was at the sink. He spoke to the back of her head. 'A fight. Was just plain stupid.'

'It was brave of you, Ronnie. And I'm proud.' Her shoulders rose. Tightened. 'The village has suffered long enough.'

He stood up and mooched around the fridge, pouring himself a mug of milk, examining the worn fridge magnet of a smiling banana that had been there for years.

Friday arrived like a snail traversing a garden and as he drove towards Calpenny's bridge, it began to rain. The only thing he could think about as both wipers slid across the glass, was his fist bouncing off McDonagh's broad chest. He might as well punch an oak tree. His knee was also full of arthritis and he knew the more he moved around, that it could give way too.

His hands rattled against the steering wheel and he gripped it harder. He drove through the village and as the rain came heavier, he clicked the wipers into a faster speed and watched people rush into huddles underneath the striped awnings of the butchers and bakers. Towards the lone traffic lights, he shifted down through his gears expecting red, but the green was steady. As he left the village, his window began to steam and he turned the heat to medium and the blower to number two, then he caught a misted glimpse of the church hall, that had four days ago stood as a wonderful place of joy, but now hunched into a mess of charred timbers. He passed through the forest. Rounded the corner. Saw McDonagh with his squad already waiting. His body went into shudders that he couldn't control. Car pulled to a stop just before the old stone bridge. He felt like he was going to vomit.

He turned off the engine. Wipers fell silent. Windscreen filled up with a dripped dream of McDonagh standing on the bridge, arms folded and a smile across his lips. He circled the gold wedding ring around his finger a couple of times, before taking it off and placing it on the dashboard.

As he stepped out of the car, a small grunt came up from his chest and lodged in his throat. He locked the car.

Pushed his shoulders back. Raised his chin up. Walked towards McDonagh and put on a show of rubbing his hands together, like he'd been waiting for it all day. Then the thoughts came to him once more, as they had on many nights in bed, of McDonagh terrorising the village and never getting caught, never getting confronted.

It rained hard.

A switch he did not even know existed clicked somewhere in his brain, as gently as a bird shifting a wing-feather. He unbuttoned his shirt. Hoped the uncontrollable nerve in his right leg wouldn't be visible through his trousers. McDonagh suggested they go over the rules, but he spat back that he didn't fight by any rules. Took off his shirt. Flung it to the ground.

He began to throw some light punches against the rain, even though he didn't know how to, just to warm up, or make it look like he knew how to warm up. As he saw McDonagh ready to speak, he interrupted and did his own talking.

'It's better you all hear this now, before we start, while you still have the chance to walk away.' His voice faltered. He tried to put some gusto into it. 'I once killed a man. With a single blow. Something they taught me in the army. So I know where to strike a man *just* right and *just* hard enough, to drop him like a stone. I'm giving out the warning now, for all those present to hear, that I'll not be held accountable for your corpse.' He looked McDonagh in the eyes. 'You're all witnesses. Obliged to tell the police what happened. As long as I give the warning it is alright. Trained killers must give the warning, it's part of their oath.'

McDonagh took off his own shirt. Revealed his bulk.

"Now hold on a second here. That's not allowed. There's rules to a fight. You can't just come in, armed with knowing how to kill a man with one blow. Sure what kind of a fair fight is that?'

Ronnie swung a hooked arm into the rain. Did it again for good measure. 'I'll tell you one more time, you better tell the police the truth, what really happened. I don't fight by rules. I only fight to the death. If I ever have to use this knowledge, to kill a man with a single strike, then I must declare it first out of courtesy and give my opponent a chance to pull out.' It was then that a pain came into his knee and he fought to stop a grimace catching his face.

One of McDonagh's men, the one with the flat nose, said then, that he wouldn't be telling the police anything. McDonagh lifted up his hands and coiled them into pummelling fists that dripped with evening rain.

The shake in his leg had stopped. He formed his own fists and held one out in front and the other down by his belly, for no reason other than he'd seen them do it in films. Then he started into a stare that bore right through McDonagh's very eyes and into whatever lay beyond.

As he waited for McDonagh to make a move, he had already decided to put all of his energy into a single fist-throw and hope that it would do some damage. *Any damage.*

The river beneath them roared, like a gale pushing through a forest of trees.

McDonagh averted his gaze then, off to the side, and suddenly dropped both fists. Raindrops bounced off the bridge all around a large, brown rat, that sat there staring at McDonagh with its thick tail curled across the wet stone.

The rat flinched. McDonagh pulled back.

Ronnie swung his entire life and breath into his fist and struck McDonagh on the forehead and McDonagh angled backwards, before falling into a sit, then slumped back onto the soaked ground. The one with the flat nose said then, that by almighty God, he had killed him.

The rat slinked off the wall and scuttled up onto McDonagh's bare chest, then just sat there like it had found a warm, familiar nest.

As he stood over McDonagh, an ache settled across his knuckles and pushed its way up through the bones of his arm and into his elbow. It was then that he picked up his shirt and pointed at each of the men in turn. 'I warned you what would happen.' He took a step forward. 'And if you don't leave the village alone, I'll be coming after you, one by one, and I'll do the same to you.'

He turned and walked back to the car. Rain dripping from his nose, his chin, the tips of his fingers. The men behind him begin to shout at the rat.

As soon as the door clunked shut, he began to shiver. He placed the heavy shirt onto the passenger seat. Put his wedding ring back on. Started the engine. The wipers cleared away the dream.

As he drove home puddles lay wide on the roads and he turned the heater up full. His white chest hair sat matted against his skin and ten thousand white pips appeared all over his body.

When he pulled into the driveway, she was at the window and before he even killed the engine she was at the front door with a forehead full of lines and a face that had aged since he last saw it. He carried the shirt with him and walked bare-chested into his house. Saw the record player in the living room. Heard the fizzle of space between songs. She got a towel. Draped it around his shoulders. They stood looking at each other with the quiet intensity of a single heartbeat. The music came on. Ruby Murray began to sing.

Softly, softly come to me
Touch my lips so tenderly
Softly, softly turn the key
And open up my heart

Then she moved in close. Put her head in the nape of his neck. She started to sway. He did too.

Handle me with gentleness

And say you'll leave me never
In the warmth of your caress
My love will live for ever and ever

So softly, softly come to me
Touch my lips so tenderly
Softly, softly turn the key
And open up my heart

Softly, softly turn the key
And open up my heart.

The Lady In the Garden

It was a hot smudge of an afternoon and long-legged field flies drifted amongst the neat gardens. Along the terrace of twelve houses there was quietness to the air, broken only by bird chirps coming across the fields or the occasional rolling hum of a car going through its gears somewhere further down the hill. Some people were gone for the day, eating ice-creams at the seaside, while others sat in their back gardens enjoying the shade and avoiding the hot indoors. Those who liked the sun lazed out front, reading a newspaper or listening to a faintly playing radio, disappearing back inside every so often for a drink.

In the kitchen of the third house, Kathleen pulled a chair to the sink and stood up onto it, taking bites of water from the tap and gasping in between. She grabbed her smooth stick of chalk and passed through the sultry hall, then out through the front door which had been wedged open to welcome cool air, a visitor that would never arrive.

She jumped off the step and knelt in the warm grass, squinting as she wrote her name across the vertical boards of the fence. A single, shaky white letter on each panel. As she paused to consider her next scrawl, Kathleen heard a low voice. She turned, expecting someone to have opened the gate and stepped into the garden, but the wood was still and the metal latch winked at her like a bright, silvery eye. She heard it again. Her blue iris pulled to a gap in the timber panels to see the lady next door sitting out in the garden in her wheelchair. Hair like suds. Glasses like swirls of liquorice. Blanketed legs poking out the bottom like sticks of rhubarb planted into frothy slippers. A wasp hovered around her bubble hair, landed amongst the nectarless curls, then took off again in zigzag flight.

'I wish I was dead.'

Kathleen pressed her face against the wood. Tried to see who the lady in the garden might be talking to. Sometimes men with hairy noses and flat caps would stop by the gate for a conversation, resting their pale hands on the wood, squinting at the sun as they spoke. Or ladies with sagging tights and curling hairdos would step in, nodding and rearranging their handbags, then fixing her blanket before they left. But the gate remained on its latch and the path was empty and grey.

'I wish I was dead.'

Kathleen watched the old shoulders rise briefly, then settle down into a long summer sigh. She thought the lady in the garden must be either talking to herself or God. She listened a moment, then held her chalk up to the fence-gap and shook it side to side, pretending to colour in the lady's hair and wishing that her chalk was blue or maybe green. She left the fence and crawled along the garden path, drawing squares and writing numbers inside them.

One. Two. Three. Four.

When she had reached ten, she leapt up. Started to hop and skip amongst them.

Cinderella, dressed in yella
went upstairs to kiss her fella
made a mistake, and kissed a snake
how many doctors did it take?

She turned at the step, moved along the path, then turned at the gate.

Mr. Taylor from the end house came idling up the road, tweed jacket hooked into his fingers and falling over one shoulder. He stopped at next door's gate and reached over, letting himself in and trying to blow his nose with a handkerchief at the same time. The lady in the garden sat unblinking and grey. Kathleen interrupted her game to kneel by the fence and pant and listen.

'How you doing, Mrs. McEldane? Thon's a warm day. I see the cows are lying down in the field.' Mr. Taylor's voice sounded like machinery that was no longer running as it should.

'What?'

'I said it's so warm the cows are lying down.'

In between dabbing his forehead and nodding, he leaned on a hip and stood like a teapot. The lady in the garden replied with words that were as soft as tall grass and few in their number.

Kathleen became disinterested and stood up to continue her game. She did ten runs of the path and sometime in between, Mr. Taylor had left and latched the gate again.

Sitting on the step for a rest, Kathleen tried to stand her stick of chalk upright. It toppled on each attempt. Rolled for the edge. As she examined its worn tip with a dusty thumb, the rumble of some distant plane swelled overhead and faces from gardens looked up to catch its snapshot against the blue satin sky. Its presence faded into warm summer hush. Kathleen heard something flick against the fence. She left her chalk upon the step and knelt down. Titled her head. The timber boards looked to her like train tracks. She paused and smiled at the thought of a mystery train choo-chooing around all of the gardens at night while people snored in their beds.

Something flicked again. She peered through the gap in the panels and saw Glenn McElroy in the next garden over. Head just visible over the far fence. He smiled and took aim, then threw something tiny that landed right in the lady in the garden's foamy hair. Glenn disappeared and the lady in the garden didn't move. Then, up bobbed Ricky Harshaw with a smile across his lips. Kathleen watched him throw and miss, his object flicking against the wood not too far from her face. She spied it in the grass and saw that it was a peanut.

Kathleen crawled along the path like a crab. Reached up to unlatch the gate. Made out onto the street, keeping low to avoid being seen by the lady in the garden. When she reached the next garden over, she crept along its path and there was Glenn and Ricky, hunkered down with their sweaty fringes hanging over a bowl of peanuts.

'What're you doing?'

'Watch this.' They sniggered. Glenn grabbed a peanut, stood up and took aim, then landed it perfectly into the lady in the garden's hair. They all watched for a reaction, but there was none.

'Don't do that,' said Kathleen.

Ricky stood up and threw his. It hit the fence. 'Missed again!'

'You're rubbish!' said Glenn.

The boys ate a peanut and Kathleen had one too, then the front door opened and there was Glenn's dad stretching and yawning with his belly poking out from under his navy t-shirt.

'What're you childer up to?'

'Just eating peanuts, dad.'

'Well, don't eat too many or you'll all end up with

the shits.' He came out and sat on the low summer-seat under the window. Put his head back against the brown sill and closed his eyes. After a few seconds, he opened them again and watched the kids sitting quietly, eating peanuts, before shifting his gaze to the lady in the garden.

'Can we all have a lolly out of the fridge, dad?'

'No.'

He scratched at his unshaven face. Crossed one leg over the other. His gaze locked onto the lady in the garden and even as the sun pushed into his eyes, still, he watched her.

'Did you offer Mrs. McEldane a nut?'

Glenn's eyes widened. 'No.'

'Right, well, away you go around and ask her if she wants a few nuts, son.'

'I'll go later on, sure. I think she's maybe asleep.'

'You'll go now.' Glenn's dad uncrossed his legs. 'I'm warning you, don't be eating all them nuts or you'll be lying up later with sore guts and your ma will blame me!'

As Glenn stood up and started to climb over the fence, his dad leaned forward and flicked a finger towards the road, 'Don't be so lazy and go around through the gate like any normal person.'

Glenn got down again, lifted the bowl of nuts, sighed, and skulked his way up the path. He opened the gate and stood out on the footpath, looking both directions and loitering like someone waiting on a lift. Kathleen and Ricky stood at the fence to watch him, while Glenn's father shook his head and made a tutting noise.

'What are you waiting on, son? Christmas?' He closed his eyes and leaned his head back against the sill. Glenn made his way along the street and into her garden. He stepped onto the grass and held out the bowl. Could see his reflection in her black liquorice glasses.

'Would you like a couple of nuts?'

She reached out and took the bowl from him, leaning in towards the nuts as though she were searching for a particular one in the pile. Her bony hand, with its aqua veins and pallid skin selected one and placed it into her wrinkled mouth. Glenn noticed three nuts in her hair, then a fourth, then watched her finger hover the bowl as if choosing another. She looked up at Glenn and nodded briefly, before shunting the bowl towards him and flinging all of the nuts into his face. He stood there with his shoulders arched and arms held out like he'd just been soaked by a bucket of water. A stray nut momentarily caught between his lips, dislodged and fell down into the grass.

Glenn began to cry. Ran back into his own garden.

'What's wrong with you?' asked his father, suddenly opening his eyes.

Glenn bawled past him and into the house. Slammed a door. His father looked to Kathleen and Ricky. 'What happened?'

'I've to go home,' said Ricky, springing to his feet. He left the garden and ran away up the street.

'Did you see what happened, Kathleen?'

'They threw the nuts at her and then she wished she was dead and so then, she just threw the nuts back at them, to make it all even.'

'Who was throwing nuts? My Glenn?'

Kathleen nodded.

Glenn's father stood up and went inside. 'Where are you, you wee shite?'

Kathleen sat for a moment, waiting, in case Glenn came back outside, then thought of her chalk and decided it was time to go home. The sun was hung high in the sky and it made her squint as she walked the length of the path. She glanced over the fence at the lady in the garden and thought she saw a smile on her pale old face. As she stepped into the street, Kathleen heard a dog barking and knew it was the tiny brown one from number seven, just by the pitch of its yelp. By the time she was in her own garden and had latched the gate, she could hear laughter, loud and rasping.

Kathleen ran to the step and picked up her chalk. It felt warm. Comforting even. The sun caught the back of her neck and stung like a slap. She glanced at her white squares on the path knowing the rains would come sometime to wash them away, then went to the fence and looked between the boards at the old shoulders rising up and down, and she listened as the sound of aged laughter filled the sultry summer air.

Milk

He woke. Propped onto an elbow. Squinted into the darkness. Listened for her breath. Outside it rained in waves of pattering, metallic-sounding droplets that glugged down drainpipes and into gulleys below.

Patricia exhaled softly.

He lay back upon the pillow, listening to her breath and the rain. For a while he was still, then put on his glasses and checked the clock.

4.07 a.m.

Walter got up and went to the bathroom where he peed for a long time. He washed his hands and stood scratching his white chest hair under the jaundiced light. He was awake and the night for him was over.

He pulled on his grey robe and went downstairs where he set the kettle to boil and readied a mug with a teabag. He used to like these small hours. Shackles of mankind lifted. Everything in the world adjourned. Every noise sharper. Purer. More amplified. He could relax back then, but now his mind was a jumble.

The kettle bubbled. Steam rose and spread briefly against the ceiling, before the button popped out. He poured water into the mug. Stirred. Dropped the teabag into the pedal-bin with the squeaky lid and winced at the sound.

At the table, he cupped his hands around the drink and listened to rain pummel the gulley outside, gurgling the depths towards unseen tunnels. Towards bulging rivers.

He sipped some tea.

Patricia hadn't lost any hair.

He held onto the hope that she wouldn't.

'Not everyone's hair falls out,' the oncologist said during that first appointment. Walter knew by the way she bristled that she hated the very idea of it. He waited for her to bring it up on their way home.

"I couldn't wear a wig." She began to cry. "I mean, it would be embarrassing. I wouldn't look like myself. People would stare at me like…like some kind of leper."

"You don't have to wear a hairpiece, love." He squeezed her hand, glad he said hairpiece instead of wig. It sounded better. Less intrusive. "Let's just take things a day at a time. Not everyone loses their hair. That's what he said."

She was a mess. Walter knew it could set her back. She might not want to leave the house for their Sunday walks together along the canal. To hold hands along the towpath. For the movies.

He couldn't take her home without doing something, so decided to stop off and buy an electric blanket. It was the only measure he could think of in the moment. They had said the shivers would come. But none had. Maybe after the second round she will get shivers, he thought, and she can use the blanket.

He yawned and brushed a crumb off the table. The bed creaked above. But no footsteps to the bathroom. He felt hungry and took out the biscuit tin, stared into it, before replacing the lid. He was hungrier than biscuits.

Walter opened a drawer as slowly and silently as he could. Carefully lifted out a silver saucepan. Grimaced as water struck the metal like tiny screams. The pouring of liquid glass. He placed it on the hob and turned on the cooker at the wall, supporting the heavy red switch with his fingertips so not to wake Patricia with the click. She needed her sleep. Sleep was healing.

He slid in four potatoes then retrieved his newspaper from the living room and read the articles he'd avoided first time around. Even read the horoscopes, although he didn't believe in astrology. *Anything* to occupy his mind. By the time his spuds were ready and he had dropped a knob of butter into their hot skins, the newspaper was finished and he ate quietly at the table.

Outside, the rain had stopped and the gulleys slowed to a gentle tap-tapping. The hospital would be calling with Patricia's results. She'd had the chemo. A follow-up scan. It had been three weeks. His robe had worked its way loose as he ate and he felt the cold creep in around his chest. He tightened it again and switched the heat on so that Patricia wouldn't wake up freezing or catch a chill.

Influenza.

Pneumonia.

Pleurisy.

They could all finish her.

He checked the time on the cooker. Four fifty-nine. It would be hours before she woke for the first medication of the day. Sometimes she stayed up a while after swallowing that rainbow of tablets, but mostly she felt nauseous and returned to bed. Patricia was sleeping more. He was sleeping less. And what if he got sick himself? The thought floated around his mind like the wispy seed from a dandelion clock. Who would look after his wife?

Walter folded his arms, feeling each bicep with a thumb and wondering what had happened to his strength over the years. Patricia used to love the strength of his embrace and they'd both laugh if he squeezed her too tight. She'd watch his rugby matches every weekend and hug him as he came off the field no matter how wet or muddy or sometimes even bloody he was. Now he did nothing and his body had sagged like a baked apple.

He entered the garage through a door off the kitchen

and tugged the string-light, then stood under its orange intensity, searching for the dumbbells he used to lift back in the day. It was cold and he pulled the door over. After searching through cupboards and having no joy, Walter remembered the car boot sale he and Patricia had gone to a couple of years back and the image in his mind of a tall fellow who was thinner than a whippet, buying the weights.

'He'll never carry them home,' Patricia had said, sipping from a Styrofoam cup, 'his arms will snap off.'

They had laughed. He hugged her close. Kissed her lips. He can still remember the smell of that perfume she used to wear. Apricots. Hint of lemon. She had so much more colour in her face back then. *More life.*

Walter reached for the string-light and his eye caught a frayed white lace, hanging from a high shelf. He took down his old trainers. Brought them through to the kitchen. The laces had lost their neat plastic tips and although the heels were worn down a little, the soles still sat like little ploughed fields of rubber. Not bad for twenty-year-old runners.

He put them on and tied the laces and walked the kitchen. They felt good. He opened the robe and let it fall to the ground. Bent forward to touch his toes. A fingertip skimmed the leather. He stood up nodding.

Walter decided then that he would go running every morning before Patricia woke. Get himself robust. Maybe even *athletic*. It would kill some time, but most importantly, settle his mind. He could squeeze her some oranges when he got back. He rifled through the laundry basket by the kitchen door and put on his paint-stained tracksuit bottoms, the ones for DIY, a vest and a red fleece, then left her a note in case she woke early. He drew a heart at the bottom with an arrow shooting through.

As he headed for the door he heard a bird chirp and stopped to listen. He wondered who heard that first chirp each day. That waking dawn. Another chirp, then another. By the time he closed the door gently and stepped outside, the chirrups had collated into rising and falling tones that resembled talking, but not yet song. Walter ambled to the end of the street where the light was faint, as though creeping through a door left ajar. The road was dark. Air damp. He turned right and began to jog.

The streetlights shone yellow puddles onto the path that guided him like glistening beacons towards the countryside. As he passed hulking silhouettes of houses, his gait was a haphazard affair of old muscles sliding over weakened tendons, but he hoped to find rhythm as he warmed. If he made it to Cullen's Bridge it wouldn't be much further to the Harrison Garden Centre, then down past the post office and round towards home again. About four miles in total.

The first real pain came only a few minutes in. His lower back. He stopped by a field-gate to stretch, bending towards rain droplets that hung from the horizontal metal bars like a thousand tiny eyes. He swished a finger through them and as he stood up again, noticed a parliament of crows on the grass, circling around the one being judged. He pictured them closing in. Decision made. Pecking the weakest to death.

At the bridge he felt a cool wind come off the river and skiff his sweating skin. He had covered a mile, maybe more. Damp lounged in the fields. Scents of leaves and morning dew and woody hedgerows had begun to cling to his body. He pictured himself arriving home, chuffed with his run. Patricia would smile and say that he smelled like outside.

He neared the Harrison Garden Centre and took a notion to run right through it. This could be his thing. To break the monotony. Running through different, unexpected places. It would involve climbing a fence and he wasn't averse to the idea, until he suspected Harrison's Dobermann would be out on patrol, so he kept on going, unintentionally increasing his pace. As he neared the post office, the stench of sweat overwhelmed everything else and he could feel imaginary crows jab his body. He stopped and bent over. Panting. A strange metallic taste sat in his mouth. As he stood there, hands leaning on thighs, he glanced up to see a trio of milk bottles on someone's doorstep. Foil lids fresh with dew.

Walter paused to look around, then opened one and gulped at it. He got halfway through the bottle before stopping himself mid-swallow. He remembered that time he had stolen an apple from a market stall. Patricia had already taken a bite, but knew something was up by the way he laughed. When he told her he had swiped it, she spat it onto the street and gave him the same warning her mother had always given her, that theft is wrong and those who steal will have another wrong visited upon them for the wrong they have committed.

He shook his head. Mumbled. 'Sure, it was only a drop of milk. No real harm done.' He took off running. Tossed the bottle over a hedge.

As he passed the post office, Walter's legs began to lose all of their strength. He could not run the last mile. It was not in him. Something in his own mind, a heaviness, dragged at him.

A car drove past. Who was it? Had they recognised him? He began to feel foolish.

His breaths slowed enough to begin walking.

That image of Patricia spitting out the apple replayed in his mind and it took a while for his breath to settle properly. In that time, morning arrived quietly, like someone entering a waiting room, sitting down to a newspaper.

Walter started jogging again, but the more he thought about Patricia, the faster he ran. As he turned onto their road, he leaned over Thompson's hedge to wretch into their garden. It felt like he was there a long time, whitening their grass. When he gathered himself enough to walk the last stretch, his throat and mouth burned at the same time.

He neared home. Saw a light on in the hall.
Maybe Patricia had woken early?
Maybe he had switched it on before he left?
He couldn't remember.

A Woman Named Celie

The priest scuffed his nose with a grey handkerchief like it was some kind of unshakable habit rather than a need, then spoke in a tone as inspiring as a spent candle. As the words drifted out over the heads of the packed attendance, the little Jack Russell dog abandoned his vigil by the coffin and pattered down the aisle to the turn of every head in the place, except for the widow, who sat in the first row with her hair in tight grey curls and a look of indifference upon her face.

After the cold, distant clunk of the chapel door, ten minutes passed before people grew bored, some whispering *that dog had the right idea* and trying their best not to laugh at a funeral.

A couple more times the door creaked open, as someone came in and sat at the back, but on the third disruption whispers rolled along the pews as the dog walked up the centre aisle and lay down by his master's coffin. Those who couldn't see, murmured that he'd probably gone out to relieve himself and those who could, tried harder to see whatever it was that he held between his teeth. He dropped it onto the worn oak floor and a hum started to rise in the room. The priest had to stop speaking and issue a *'quiet please.'*

The widow sighed. One hand rested upon the other in her lap, with a finger slowly tapping the pallid skin. Her dress was bright blue with hyacinth flower-prints and she stood out against the black mourners like a moonbow.

The dog began scratching the old floor with his front paws like he would quite like to bury something, and as people looked to the widow for intervention, she ignored them and examined a fingernail. A man sitting in the front row with a red face, drew a breath and got up, smiling awkwardly as he lifted the dog and sat back down with it on his lap. The priest paused for a drink of water, before continuing to speak like a distant foghorn that would never cease.

The little dog growled and the man tried poking and shushing it, but as the dog turned to look him in the eye, to growl louder, the man's face lost its authority and took on an expression of fear.

'He's probably lookin' that trinket he brought in,' said the woman in the black dress beside him. 'Hold on.' She got up and did a crouch-walk. Picked up the item. Reversed her oversized-behind onto the pew again. She saw, as her husband also leaned in, that it was pitted and brown. A wooden smoking pipe. She offered it to the dog and he took its tip in his mouth like a regular person would, but still continued to growl.

'I think he wants down,' she said.

They glanced along the row for some help from the widow, but she sighed again and her eyelids seemed to open and close more slowly than a person's should. They could feel the eyes in the rows behind them bore into the backs of their heads, so the man released the Jack Russell. It strolled to the coffin. Stood pipe in mouth. Scratched a paw against the wooden plinth. The priest gave the man with the red face a glare of disdain and the man wished he had never taken anything to do with anything.

Just as the priest seemed to get back into his verbal meander, the dog left the pipe on the floor and began to move along the front row, sniffing each person in turn. People smiled. Low voices hummed like a bow across a cello. Some of the gazes looked to the widow, who seemed to be attending a different funeral than everyone else.

When the dog stopped at an old fellow in a tweed cap whose face was sucked in around the mouth, it placed two front paws onto the pew and stuck its nose against the man's trouser leg.

'What're you after?' asked the old fellow, patting the dog's head.

The dog sniffed and snorted, until the man put a wrinkled hand into his pocket and pulled out a small red tin with *Peterson Irish Flake* etched across it. The animal watched him. Head cocked to one side.

'You want this?'

It barked once.

The priest had had enough and stopped his eulogy. 'What is going on down there?'

'Don't know what he's after,' the old fellow chuckled through his gummy smile.

'Will you take him outside, please? I am trying to conduct a funeral service here.'

'Right you be.' The old fellow nodded and made to get up.

The dog returned to the coffin where it lifted the pipe, then waited for the old fellow to catch up. The old fellow kneeled. 'You're lookin' some tobacco? Is that it?'

As the priest continued, the old fellow opened his tin and pulled out a pinch of wiry tobacco, before stuffing it into the pipe with his forefinger. The dog looked at him and he looked back. The dog barked from the side of his mouth.

The man heard a stutter in the priest's words and peered up from behind the coffin to give a wave. 'All under control.'

No further than four feet away, the widow's shoulders rose briefly and deflated again. The priest gave her a dirty look not fit for a chapel and she replied with nothing more than a defiant stare.

The old fellow pulled out a lighter, paused to shake his head in disbelief, then lit the tobacco. He returned to his seat and observed the dog sitting content by his master's coffin and ignoring everyone in the place. The dog sat listening to the sermon as puffs of smoke rose up to the vaulted ceiling to join the candle grease and memories of spent tears.

It was then that a young lad in the third row, with black sideburns that would have made Elvis proud, pointed at the smoke and said, 'Look, the Indians are coming.' The fellow beside him smiled and repeated it to the person beside him, and before long, the chapel became a complex web of people nodding towards the smoke puffs and whispering to each other.

By the time the laughter spread, people had started to stand, to catch glimpse of the dog smoking his pipe. Some stepped into the aisle to get a better view. The priest stopped talking and came right out of the pulpit and onto the chapel floor to see for himself what was going on. His face boiled into rich crimson. As he grabbed for the pipe, off the dog ran down the aisle. He looked to the widow, who calmly investigated something inside her purse, and as the place erupted into an unholy laughter, someone held open the heavy chapel door for the little terrier to escape.

When the service was finally over, a few men lifted the coffin and mourners fell in behind. They left the chapel, trickling the narrow path towards the tall gates of the cemetery where the sky hung low and grey. By the time the swell of bodies had gathered by the graveside, the widow came sauntering down the hill with her flower-print dress catching in the wind.

People looked for the dog. Could not see him. The priest stood with his hands by his side, one holding a bible, the other doing nothing.

When the widow arrived, she sat on a seat reserved for inconsolable family members whose legs no longer held the power to stand. Took a book from her handbag. Read quietly about a woman named Celie. The priest repeated things he had already said about God and souls and mansions in heaven. Announced a hymn. As people sang and the coffin entered the earth, the widow licked a thumb and turned a page.

The song floated and lingered there in the space above them, as the crowd filed past the graveside and the widow closed the book in her lap to let people shake her hand or bend for an unwanted embrace. The line eventually broke out. Men loosened their ties. Lit cigarettes. Headed for the gate.

Some glimpsed the dog among distant headstones. The gravedigger waited for his time.

When it was only the widow and the priest left, he placed a hand on her shoulder. 'Take as long as you need, Muriel.'

In between grey clouds, white seams appeared, like

fabric pulling slowly apart. The gravedigger began shovelling in what he had only recently taken out. Muriel opened her book. Listened to the gentle thuds of dirt. When the hole was full and the gravedigger had it level, he bowed his head and walked off with his hands in his pockets.

Muriel got up from the chair. Stepped onto the soil. Her short-heels sank. Feet started to kick and stamp, spraying soil out onto the surrounding grass. She jabbed a knee upward and flicked out her shin, then smiled and did the same with the other leg. She heard her tights split along one calve and paused to look at her blue veins, before continuing her dance back and forth along his grave. She finished with a flurry of the Charleston, until the neat brown rectangle was no longer neat and the breaths heaved from her body.

She grinned and flung her head back to catch the sky finally splitting and the sun's grand yellow coming through. Felt her cheeks warm. Closed her eyes. When she opened them again, the little dog was at her side.

He looked at her once, dropped the pipe onto the ground, then sat by his master's headstone and began to whine.

Christmas

It seemed everywhere he looked there were trees going someplace. Trees crisscrossed with blue twine, sailing by on trailers. Trees slumped across car roofs. People blurred into a scurry of earmuffs and scarves as they trailed fresh cut pines or spruces across town, puffing out half-frozen breaths like vessels upon a sea.

Jimmy Doherty couldn't afford a tree ten or even twenty years ago and couldn't afford one now. Usually, he decided this would be the year he went out and cut his own, but same as before, it was dishonest and he wouldn't steal from another man's land. Jimmy Doherty could barely fuel his fire or his stomach, so a Christmas tree, although high on his list of wants, was last on his list of needs.

As December nestled in, winter took everything in its grip and the town slowly changed into a wonderland of decorations, colourful lights and festivity. People sang carols in the street. Hounded by darkness and cold. Shops burst onto the pavement. The pub bustled behind sparkling trees in its wood-gridded windows. People went mad and rushed at everything, but Jimmy was just the same old Jimmy.

When Christmas Eve arrived Jimmy wandered out to the backyard and stood hands on hips, observing his four chickens. One remained still as though frozen solid. The others pecked at nothing and bobbed as they walked. All were thin, for this year had been particularly difficult, but still, one would have to be selected and he watched them for some time before deciding which would be his meal the following day.

After the bird was plucked and prepared, Jimmy needed some festivity. He rooted in the bottom drawer for the giant pair of rust-stained scissors that squeaked as they cut, then went down to the bottom of the yard where Mrs. Gillespie's bushes sprawled over the boundary. For years he had asked her permission until eventually she scowled and told him to just go ahead in future. He snipped three sprigs from her holly tree and went back inside.

Placing holly was no simple task. He dangled a sprig from the living room light. Set one on the window sill. Another on the hearth. He sat down then, tapping a finger against his trouser leg, before standing into the kitchen doorway for a different angle. He placed one at either end of the hearth, then moved the window sill sprig up onto the curtain pole so it could still be seen whenever the curtains were closed. He stood nodding. The room had a look of Christmas about it alright.

Mid-morning approached upon the crest of winter's rasp and Jimmy sat in his old armchair, the one with the gnawed leg where Mrs. Gillespie's dog had chewed it one summer afternoon. His gaze drifted from the curling leaves of holly to the window, where a delicate waterfall of snow was already coming down. He had always loved a snowy Christmas as a boy, but a tighter chill to the air meant an already shortened supply of firewood becoming even shorter. He considered lighting the fire, but knew his wood would be gone in no time. Evening would draw in along with a further drop in temperature and Jimmy would be sat with no orange glow to stare at.

A muffled thud-thud came to his door.

Jimmy rose from the chair as quickly as his old body would allow and said, 'right you be,' to no-one.

The smiling lady wore a pair of thick mauve mittens with matching hat and scarf. 'Merry Christmas Mr. Doherty! Just dropping this off. A wee gift from everyone at St. Martin's church.' She handed him a small basket.

'Ach you're a wee dear.' The air nipped at his face. He coughed.

'Looks like we're in for a white Christmas!'

Before he could think what to say or do, she stepped forward and gave him a hug. Then she was off up the path.

'Thanks so much!' he called after her. 'And Merry Christmas to you too!'

Jimmy closed the door and went back inside to see. As he carefully unwrapped the hamper, he became a little choked and had to steady himself. It was the fourth year they had done this. There were some pickles, bread, a pound of butter, two packets of biscuits, and a pint of milk still cold. Three bramley apples, some teabags and a jar of cranberry sauce. A tin of peas. Some carrots. He lifted out a small bottle of port. Looked forward to drinking its warmth, but didn't notice *non-alcoholic* printed small on the label.

Along with the food was a white envelope with some words written on it. Mrs. Gillespie would have to read it. And a snip of mistletoe. Real mistletoe like they had when he was a boy.

Jimmy put the things away in his bare cupboards and left the mistletoe atop his fireplace. Putting on his gloves, made from old brown socks with finger holes cut out, and the worn cap that had belonged to his father, he pocketed the card and a bramley apple and went round to Mrs. Gillespies.

Snow fluttered down. Light yet heavy at the same time. When Mrs. Gillespie opened the door, heat exploded over him.

'Jimmy! What are you doing out in this weather?'

'I got this card,' he pulled it from his pocket, 'and

wondered if you might read it for me.'

'Get in here now, before one of us catches pneumonia!' He kicked his boots against the doorstep. Went inside.

While Mrs. Gillespie searched for her reading glasses, Jimmy warmed himself by the fire and patted her dog Sherbet.

'What's that lovely smell? Turf is it?'

'Tis. Ma son brought two sackfuls the other day.' Mrs. Gillespie sat down. 'You can have a log if you want.'

'Thanks so much. That's too kind.' He reached into his pocket. 'Here, I brought you a Bramley.'

She took the apple and turned the envelope in her fingertips. 'It's a card, saying *Glad Tidings to All Men* on the front. Printed not written.'

'How do you know it's a card?'

'Sure that's all people send at Christmas time is cards!' She tutted. Opened it. 'There's a message inside from the reverend. And a five pound note.'

'There never is a five pound note! What does the message say?'

She handed him the money. Sherbet's ears perked up in hope that it was a prize for her. Mrs. Gillespie read aloud. *'I hope this hamper and gift will help you have a merry Christmas indeed and you are most welcome at our service on Christmas morning at eleven o'clock.'*

'Are you going to that service?' he said, turning the five pound note in his hands.

'No, sure doesn't ma son come to pick ma up every

Christmas morning and take ma away for the day?'

'Right enough. Well, I won't see you then, so have a merry Christmas and make something nice with the bramley.'

Jimmy took the card and headed for the front door. She followed him out. He loitered on the front step, caught between wanting to ask. Not wanting to offend.

'So, would you give me a lump of yer turf?'

She tutted him again. 'It's out in the shed. And I've knitting to finish here by tomorrow. A jumper for ma nephew. Will throw it over the hedge into your yard later.'

'Thank you.'

Sherbet came to the threshold with the bramley in her mouth just as Mrs. Gillespie shut the door. Jimmy made out into the snow, a five pound note in his pocket and some joy in his heart. He walked a short distance to the shop, where he bought a tin of corned beef, Jammie Dodgers and some toilet roll. He saw a large box of matches on offer for two thirds the true price, so bought them too. At the counter he spied a box of huge magnifying glasses. Bought one for a pound.

When he got into the house, winter had broken in. Stolen every last remnant of warmth. Jimmy set his groceries on the kitchen bench and went into the back yard to check for his turf. Nothing but white and sparkle. He wrestled the lock on the shed door and stepped in to inspect the wood. There wasn't nearly enough. He patted his hands together before going out into the street.

Snowflakes fell faster. Thicker. The streets had already changed from something familiar to a new world that was smooth and bright and pretty. By the time he reached the grassy fields, they slept under a luxurious blanket of beautiful white. The air had a sharper bite to it and he could feel shivers starting to drum inside him. He crossed two fields before turning around. Nothing could be found in this weather. Jimmy needed to go home, but needed wood. He headed back towards town, to the Jersey Timber Yard, but it was closed. He paused for breath. Scraped snow from the fence. Sucked it for a drink.

Passing the butchers with bulging turkeys hung by their feet in proud display, an idea entered his mind. He cut down a narrow lane. Into the back entrance of the supermarket. Sure enough there were wooden pallets, piled high and capped with snow. He examined them. Made his way back up the lane.

As he entered the supermarket it was packed beyond packed. People fussed and grabbed and moved under the jingling sound of Christmas music. The beep-beep of the checkouts chattered through the air. Jimmy asked a young girl with spiked hair if he could speak with the manager. Without hesitation she spoke into some microphone and her voice squawked over the music for the manager to come to the checkouts.

Within the minute a tall, slim man, wearing a check shirt and a red Christmas tie appeared. Beneath his beard came a wonderful smile.

'What can I do for you, sir?'

'I see you have a broken pallet out the back there,' he pointed, 'looks pretty bad. Beyond repair I'd say. Would you mind if I took it home? Just for firewood.'

'No problem!' He slapped Jimmy on the back. Gave him the friendliest grin. 'You'd be doing me a favour! Go right ahead.'

As Jimmy thanked him and made for the exit, two girls in Santa hats stood holding a large tub.

'Thank you for your custom today! Would you like a sweet?'

'I never bought anything, love. So it wouldn't be right. Thanks anyway.'

'Sure it's Christmas!' They each shoved sweets into his hands.

Outside snow billowed at him like fresh hung sheets, catching his eyelashes, dipping into the space between his bare neck and collar. Jimmy blew into his hands. Ate a sweet. The welcome burn of a brandy ball.

When he walked around back to lift his prize, it was surprisingly heavy. Reminded him of the time he had helped Mrs. Gillespie rearrange her furniture and spent two weeks in bed with a sore back. Jimmy hauled the pallet onto his shoulder and carried it through milky streets, stopping every so often to wheeze and wince, the image of a burning fire spurring him on. Towards home it became too much and he fell. Some youths passed by.

Laughed. Pelted him with snowballs.

By the time he reached home his body ached and his shoulder felt like an axe had been swung into it. Jimmy dropped the pallet in his back yard and leaned against the wall for some time, just breathing. He looked up. The entire sky was falling. He took into it with a hatchet and along with the pain came a sense of relief that he had enough firewood to make it through Christmas Day.

He glanced briefly. Still no turf.

Inside, the house was freezing. Breath visible. Body shivering. And he sometimes wished Mrs. Gillespie's heat would somehow find its way through the wall.

Jimmy arranged some wood and paper and lit the fire. Sat by it a long time. Waited for winter's sting to loosen from his face, before warming enough to edge back into the gnawed chair. As night drew in and the snow died down, Jimmy took out his new magnifying glass. The book he lifted was without the first few pages or a front cover, so he had no name for it, but as he read by the flicker of a cosy firelight, he liked its story of an orphan boy who dared ask for more food.

◈ ◈ ◈

On Christmas morning Jimmy awoke with excitement stirring inside and the pains of an old man hanging over him. He would have a full meal today and the house was nicely festive with sprigs of holly and even mistletoe.

While some tea brewed Jimmy stood looking out the window. It wasn't snowing anymore. The ground still chalky white. He poured a mug and sat in the gnawed chair. Hovered the magnifying glass over the reverend's invite. It took his mind back to when he used to attend church those years ago. There and then as the hot taste of tea roused his insides, he decided to go. He didn't own many clothes so would just have to go as he would go. People would say, look at him come to worship in his rags, but rags were all he had.

The church was much as he remembered it. A simple kind of grand. New red carpet in the entrance. Jimmy was welcomed with a warm handshake and unexpectedly someone knew him by name. He didn't think he would be nervous, but as he shuffled along the pew and sat down, something about the smell of the old wood, brought memories to his mind, of sideways glances, judgement of his clothes, and hygiene. He settled during the sermon, which was about celebrating the true reason for Christmas, until the collection plate came round and the unease returned. Shame burned down through his face in deep crimson, along his neck and chest. Nestled into the pit of his stomach.

He remembered this feeling. Not being able to afford anything to put in the collection plate. Now, as it came along the line, hands criss-crossing from smile to smile, Jimmy emptied his pocket of the two single-pound notes he had to his name. He felt their reassurance. Rubbed them slowly together. When the basket lined with crimson velvet came in his lap, Jimmy stared at the coins and notes. Gulped. Placed his two notes in and passed it to the next person in line.

At the end, the reverend gave an address for everyone to close their eyes. He said all year long they prayed for other people and today he wanted them to pray for themselves, it's time for you he said, to realise that charity does sometimes begin at home.

Jimmy prayed, then left.

Padding home, through the crunching, shifting snow, he watched children play in the streets. Pelting. Throwing and rolling. One child tried desperately to ride a new bicycle but the weather would not allow it.

The house was cold again. He went through to the back yard and briefly swept the ground with a foot. No sign of his turf. She had forgotten. Accepting he would be out scavenging for wood tomorrow again, he decided to enjoy his day.

Jimmy lit the fire and listened to its spit and crackle as he put the chicken into the oven. He peeled two carrots. Diced them. Opened a can of peas. After he had set some spuds to boil, he took down the tray from above the cupboards and set out a knife and fork. Poured a glass of port. When the food was ready, he took the tray through to the living room and sat by the fire with the meal in his lap. For a moment he thought about Mrs. Gillespie at her son's house, sitting at the table with her family. Nephews laughing. Playing with their toys. Plates piled high with food. He raised a glass to her. To them all. Took a sip.

Jimmy listened to carols on the radio and hummed along as he chewed. Heat from the fire found its way out to embrace the room. In the evening, snow fell for an hour. He drank tea and sang to himself, then went to bed warmed, nourished and filled with spirit.

◈　　　　　　◈　　　　　　◈

On Boxing Day morning he reckoned a walk in the fields to search for more firewood might be a sensible thing to do before more snow came. So he put on his old sock gloves and cap and ventured into the cold. He climbed a wire fence. Crossed some fields of melting white where he found two planks of wet wood, that if dried out could burn in his fire the very best. In the next field he kept close to the hedgerow. Watched robins flit among the snowy branches. They made him smile and he wished he had something to feed them. It was then that he saw a grand house across the way. And a man emerge. Dragging a Christmas tree the length of his garden before dumping it over the fence. Jimmy waited for him to disappear back inside his house. Made his way over.

If he took it home, it would not be stealing. The man must have enjoyed its worth. Jamming his two pieces of damp wood into one armpit, Jimmy grabbed the tree's trunk and began to trail it through the fields. Snow gobbled at his prize. By the time he reached home and pulled it into his living room, Jimmy deliberated on whether or not to chop it into firewood.

Then his mind returned to his years as a boy and he knew what he wanted to do. He rummaged around in his shed for a bucket. Found one with a crack down the side that might hold it steady. After digging some snowy soil from the garden, Jimmy brought the tree into his living room and placed it in the corner. He stood a moment. Arms folded. Nodding. It had been decades.

He had a notion then. Searched through kitchen cupboards and drawers. Sighed.

When he knocked Mrs. Gillespie's door, she answered with her hair in curlers. 'Jimmy. I'd invite you in, but people would talk. I'm not dressed properly here.' She tugged at the skin on her neck.

'No problem! Did you have a nice Christmas?'

'I did. What can I do for you?'

'Would you have any silver foil at all?'

'Hold on.' She closed the door over. Came back. Handed him the roll. Sherbet jumping up at it.

'I don't need all that. Hold on.' He tore a piece. 'Thanks a million. Oh, and would you still give me some of yer turf?'

She gave him a look of annoyance. Nodded. 'I'll go this very minute.'

The instant Jimmy got into the house, he worked at the foil, fashioning it into the shape of a rugged, dishevelled star. He placed it on top of the tree and stood back smiling. Gaze drifted to the window, where a log of turf glanced over the hedge.

A Quarter Yellow Sun

On Sundays he wears it with a certain pride. Saving the money took time but eventually there is enough. When the new suit arrives it gives him a lift. He walks with spirit. A smile drawn full. The Harris Tweed filters positivity directly into his skin.

Now as he brushes, then hangs it neatly by the bed, it remains his only suit. Everything else packed up and ready.

It is January, cold and fresh. Frost attacks his doorstep this time of year and he rises early, salting it, for fear of the postman or milkman slipping.

Tomorrow will be the day. Wednesday. He walked the two mile route last week to observe the goings on at that time of the morning. Who is around. Who will know him.

The time is set. Six o'clock. His mother always insisted

he rise at a decent hour. Not to waste the day. It stays with him over the course of his life.

In the afternoon he visits Frank the barber for a trim and tidy. Frank recalls some anecdote about two donkeys fighting in a field. It makes everyone laugh at the time but doesn't seem much funny anymore.

It is evening now. Darkness of winter settling in like sorrow. He walks to the old dresser. Lifts a brown leather case, still in good condition, flips it open. Stares at the medal inside.

Images wander his mind. Soldiers. Spreading out. Darting and stopping under fire.

Men fall to the mud. Bullets split them like poisoned rain. The familiar boom of a grenade.

He sets the leather case down again.

Before supper both shoes are spit-shined to perfection and placed beneath the hanging suit.

Everything is prepared.

As he eats alone at the table, salt and pepper mills for company, hail patters the window. He sighs. Rain is the one thing he does not want for tomorrow.

His meat is full of gristle, so he leaves most of it.

The clock sounds different. When he glances, both hands waver at four. Twitching. Trying to tick. He rustles in the drawer of miscellany and finds a couple of batteries. One is a dud. The other gets it going again.

In bed he lies still, in the darkness, and the sound of winter's fingertips tap-tapping at the window helps close his eyes.

He sleeps, he rises. Brushes the suit one last time before putting it on. As he crooks his tie into place and smoothes some wax into his greyed hair, he does the one thing that still remains. With pride, he pins the medal onto his chest.

It is time.

Winter's breath greets him at the front door. No rain. He loosens a handful of salt onto the frozen step and heads out into fading darkness. The iron gate groans as he gently ushers it closed. Pauses a moment to listen. Nothing.

He begins to walk the route, passing widower Crowe's first. A light is on but blinds all drawn. He crosses the street to McKee's Timber Yard where a rusted, flaking warning of *Guard Dog* has engrained itself onto the spike-topped gate. He passes houses still in slumber. The streetlights hum but soon they will switch off. At the corner, the Cellar Pub welcomes him into town, a line of frosted empty kegs sitting outside, waiting for morning collection.

He turns left. Puffs of breath linger momentarily behind him. Ears numb. Face a subtle crimson. He watches the breadman pull a towering casket down from the lorry and into the shop. The wheels scrape and squeal. Like the sharpening of bayonets.

He presses on. The bank is closed, everyone's money resting safely. Battered shutters of metal protect the shop rows, ready to be racketed up out of sight for another day.

Delicate pinches of ice cling to his shoes, but he cannot falter to clean them.

Bricked up buildings. Splintered doors. The church in gloom. Spire goring the sky.

Then nothing but the road.

Streetlights off. Morning light rising all around. Pastel fields border the dark asphalt. Unkempt edges protruding like iced lances. A papery mist hangs in the distance so scant it almost isn't there. Rugged fences of barbed wire and gnarled timber accompany him along the final stretch.

The road becomes a junction. His heart locks into the rhythm of each stride.

Bom. Bom. Bom-bom-bom. Bom-bom.

His stride is perpetual now. Across the quiescent, sparkling road and onto the frigid grass without any shift in his step. The grass grows taller. Scratching his knees.

He stamps hard. Rhythmically. Can hear the drums.

Bom. Bom. Bom-bom-bom. Bom-bom.

Bom. Bom. Bom-bom-bom. Bom-bom.

Winter's raw exhale flogs his face and body. Rutted stones of the shore jab into his feet as he crosses uneven ground and into the lake.

Men fell around him.

Bom. Bom. Bom-bom-bom. Bom-bom.

It is all on his shoulders as he marches that fearless

march down into the icy, numbing water. In the distance, a quarter yellow sun straddles the horizon and somewhere birds began to sing.

The Wooden Hill

It is around the time of my brother Doug's firstborn that your mind begins to slide. We call in at weekends for a cup of tea. You are still on your feet. Still cooking. Still managing to be human.

'What do you think we should call the child?' says Doug. That's how it starts.

'Patricia.' You smile. 'I like Patricia.'

The following week he asks again and the expression on your face, that surprise, as though it is the first time you have been asked, tells us something about your demise.

'Simon.'

Other weeks you have to be pressed. 'I don't know.' Your thoughts can't fight through the fog. 'What will you call him?'

'We had been thinking, Hercules.' My brother Doug

acts serious. His wife smiles. You study them a moment. Grin. Still human.

You go through a raft of names and it humours us all to hear what you will come up with next, for if you can't find humour in unfortunate situations then what can you do.

'Cybil.'

'Elizabeth.'

'George.'

'William.'

'Roger.'

'Patricia.'

'Linda.'

My brother goes through a list too, on the occasions you ask him.

'Samson.'

'Alawishes.'

'Ludwig.'

As time passes, you spend more time in the armchair. Barely move. Whenever Doug goes into the kitchen to prepare some tea, you lean towards his pregnant wife and squint.

'Do you do the dishes at home? He has you well looked after. You better not give him any bother.' You don't have a mean bone in your body, but you are drifting away into a distant grey sea.

Before all that. Before we all became adults with girlfriends or wives, or children of our own, us three boys used to visit you every Sunday. Clive the eldest. Then Doug. Then me.

Among the bubbling and steam and clink-clink of culinary implements, you fussed, but did so quietly. With a competence that resembled grace.

You'd hold a lid over the tilt of a draining saucepan. Shuffle hot sweet cabbage onto a chipped plate. Smother it with foil. Slide it into the oven. With an old knife, you'd prod inside the huge pot. Everything would be ready soon.

You would sometimes hum lines from Elvis Presley songs, before one of us boys came in and you laughed through embarrassment.

In the living room, we'd watch Bonanza or The Waltons, waiting for the drone of an open oven door.

When the spuds were ready you drained the pot and deftly swept through the potatoes with a blunt knife to peel away their soft skins. An army of plates crammed onto the small countertop. Heaped high with food and rising, mini-whirls of steam.

'Right.' That was your call.

'Get your salt and butter.' The instructions.

Everyone knew the words intimately. Couldn't do without them. I was the youngest and still liked my beef cut into tiny pieces. I was no longer the age to warrant it, yet you did it all the same. The tenderness in that simple act.

By the time each faded ceramic plate held nothing but

smears, the open fire cajoled us towards sleep and no matter how many times I was told not to do it, I still licked my plate clean.

I wouldn't say you stopped making Sunday dinner all of a sudden, but it happened fairly quickly all the same. The food became scant. You would forget to turn the oven off. At that stage my father started going two or three times a day to make your meals. Keep you living.

Around the time Doug's first daughter is born, the doctor visits. Gives you a quiz.

'Can you tell me who the prime minister is?'

'Do you know what day it is?'

'Do you know what year it is?'

You get some of them right. Then a month later, same quiz. You fail miserably.

Weight begins to fall away from your face. Your hair becomes limp, scraggy like old spaghetti. You grow so thin, that eventually, as you lie curled under the hospital blankets, you cannot speak or move and they have to come and turn you from one side to the other every hour or so to prevent bed sores and maybe even to help you feel normal. You are small. Foetal. I want to cradle you in my arms the way you did when I was a child. Your body refuses their drips and fluids. They wait on you to die. We all do. It is inhumane. It is what it is.

You die on a Thursday, in the early hours.

We meet at your house that morning. Myself and Doug arrive close together. Dad is already there, brewing tea.

'How are you holding up, Dad?' says Doug.

'I'm alright. Do yis want tea?'

'Yep.'

'What about the undertaker and all that?' I say. 'Do you want one of us to go with you?'

'It's done and all. I went to see him this morning first thing.'

'Who did you go to?'

'Mullins. He was a nice man, really genuine.'

'Did he try the hard sell on you?'

'I just told him she was a simple woman and would have a simple coffin, you know what I mean?'

I nod. It feels true. You were an unassuming woman. Humble even.

Doug sips his tea. 'Is there anything you need us to do?'

'There is one thing. You see this bit of wallpaper here?' Dad steps into the hallway. 'If we could get a piece somewhere just to tidy it up?'

The door opens. In comes Clive, carrying a look of solemn. 'Alright Daddy? Sorry about Granny.'

'Thanks son, sure we'd been waiting anyway. At least she isn't suffering anymore.'

'Aye, that's right.'

'I was just saying there about this wallpaper, if we could get another border, try and fix it up.'

'What happened that?' Clive seems the most upset, but then I suppose he is the eldest. Knew you longer than me and Doug.

'I don't know son, it's been like that a long time. It's just, everyone will see it as soon as they come through the door. It's only the border, we should be able to tidy that up alright. Here, take this twenty quid and see what you can get.'

Clive stays. Doug and me take a photo of it and head out.

'Where are we gonna get this wallpaper?' says Doug.

'There's a place up Union Street might do it, we'll try there.'

The car squeals as it moves off.

'You need a new fan-belt.'

'Aye, I know.'

A short drive to the edge of town. We stand in the wallpaper shop, grief circling us with its broad dark feathers. Nothing matches. When we speak to the lady at the counter she is very helpful and we end up in the basement looking through old boxes. In the gloom. And dust. We find a border that is similar to yours. Nip into Watson's for some polo-mints. When we stick it on, it is not perfect. But is tidy.

'I'm not sure what to do with the body,' says Dad. 'Do you think she'd want to come home for the two days or what?'

'I don't know dad, if she doesn't come home where else would she be?' Clive shuffles one foot to the other.

'Well she would just be in the funeral parlour, they

have a room, you know what I mean?'

'Aye I see.'

'Maybe I'll leave her there tonight and then bring her home tomorrow night for one last night in her own house?'

'Whatever way you want to play it.'

Dad winces. 'But then, I'd kind of be afraid to bring her home and the body be here on its own. What if somebody broke in? A burglar.'

Such a thought. You dead. And a burglar.

'Sure, we could stay if you want?' I say.

'Would you?'

'Aye.'

'Well that would maybe do then. I'll bring her home tomorrow night for the last night in her own house and you can stay?'

'That'll do.'

We drink tea in the house we visited all of our lives. People come. Eat sandwiches. We bond. It strikes me how safe this place is. Back when mum and dad separated, your little terraced home was our constant. Our one place of normality.

You were great at giving us jobs to keep us occupied. Chopping sticks in the back yard with an old hatchet. Shoving the circling blades of a push-mower through your grass.

You come home the following day. We have to leave the room when the undertakers bring in your body.

Then there you are. Dad has chosen a yellow dress. Your favourite colour.

You don't look like yourself. Lips sealed shut in a strange expression. You are so thin.

That night two of us sleep upstairs. I think about you trying to climb the wooden hill to your bed each night. Your frail body. You must have struggled.

The rooster next door wakes us at dawn. How you stuck that your whole life I'll never know.

On the day of the funeral, people cram inside your little house. It rains hard outside.

I stand beside Dad. As we sing the hymn, his body shakes. Trying with all its might to cry. Trying with all its might not to cry. The muscles in his face harden. Jaw clenches.

As we stand in your house filled with mourners, you lying there in the wooden box, I look at the fire and search for a blaze where there is none.

When I was younger you used to let me clean it out and light it. All from scratch.

I brushed out the grate. Pulled out the pan of spent ash. Took it outside to the metal silver bin. I'd start with crumpling balls of newspaper. Spread them across the grate. Then sticks. Then coal. It's all about the layers. That's what you taught me. Then the glass in the door of the fire needs to be rubbed with newspaper. Does a great job removing the soot. Black scorches.

Twist a piece of newspaper. Light it from the gas

cooker. Carry it in carefully. Get that bed of newspaper going first, then the sticks start to crackle. Flames begin to hum. Close the door and lock it.

The service finishes. We carry your coffin out and the sun appears. Faces tilt upwards like flowers seeking just a little more life.

I see sombre expressions in the street. A gathering of those who appreciate you. They mean a lot to me. I'm sure they mean the same to my brothers. To Dad.

You are ninety years old.

I hope that when I go, for we all have to die, that you will be there on the other side, a younger version of yourself, your best self.

I will go into the kitchen. There you will be with your wonderful smile.

'Here, take these.'

'What are they, granny?'

'Seeds.' Your hand will cup my shoulder. 'Me and you are going to grow some tomatoes.'

We will push them down into the soil. Place the pots onto the window sill. You will let me give them their first drink and together we will watch them grow.

Acknowledgments

I would like to thank those that encouraged me on this journey. As always, Katie Guiney. An excellent editor, wife and mother. My family and friends, for their love and inspiration. My mum who first motivated me to read by choosing visual, witty and imaginative books like Stig of the Dump, The Twits, The Beano and The Dandy.

Bill Tinley and past members of The Newman Writers Group. Miranda Dickinson for championing my writing. Matt Hall for a superb cover image. To my editor, Sean Campbell, for helping me make these short stories the best they could be. To Chris, Adam and everyone at Epoque Press. Special thanks also to the Northern Ireland Arts Council and Damian Smyth for their unwavering support. And to the numerous literary journals and publications that have published my work in the past.

Vera the cat. For encouraging me to take catnaps. Rest my brain.

Uncle Booger. For encouraging me to get out running. Clear my brain.

Bernie Meegan. For the duck eggs. Protein to feed my brain.

Eoin Smullen for Pat's Mustard!

My beautiful daughter, Scout, who brings us joy every day.

And lastly, to you dear reader, thank-you for reading my words.